The Bogeyman Next Door

Trust No One

Alex Dean

TREBOR & TAYLOR PUBLISHING

First Paperback Edition: August 2014
Printed in the United States of America

The publisher is not responsible for websites (or their content) that are not owned by the publisher.
eBook   ISBN 978-0-9905281-0-4
Paperback   ISBN 978-0-9905281-1-1

Bogey - A person or thing that causes fear or alarm.

Praise for Alex Dean's
Alexis Fields Thrill Series

RESTRAINING ORDER

"It's everything you've ever wanted in a who-dun-it!" Readers will be "pulled in" and held "captive" by this engaging read. Alex Dean's art of storytelling is quite evident in this timely thriller."

THE BOGEYMAN NEXT DOOR

Alex Dean's "The Bogeyman Next Door" is a riveting read that will keep readers on the edge of their seat from beginning to end! It's full of action, suspense, and great attention to detail. I am definitely a fan."

-Jennifer Banks, Pro Blogger

PROLOGUE

MARKED FOR DEATH...

THE FOUR MEN shuddered with fear in the back of the black Cadillac Escalade as it turned onto Mulholland Drive. Their faces remained covered, their mouths and hands bound. They winced and groaned with the notion that death could now be imminent. Then one of the kidnapped men, figuring he had just minutes left to live, hurled forward and delivered a wild and swift kick, brazenly connecting with the side of the driver's face.

The unsuspecting blow startled the driver. His adrenaline pumping now, he twisted his body and turned his anger toward the backseat.

"I'm gonna kill you, you son of a bitch!" he yelled as the looming hunk of metal came to an abrupt halt. Suddenly, he and his accomplice fiercely flung open their doors and jumped out.

The Escalade sat motionless, idling in front of the vacant house near the end of the block. The ramshackle two-story was next door to the home of Alexis Fields, who, after narrowly escaping her disturbed ex, recently relocated (along with her dog, Max, a brown and white Shih Tzu), from her hometown of Madison, Wisconsin, to Lake Park, Illinois, in search of a new life and career as a medical intern.

But there was danger lurking here tonight.

The driver and his cohort paused for a tense beat and stealthily scanned the area. There could be no witnesses, they thought. None to tell what they had seen or heard. But there *was* someone in the bushes, peering from a distance. He'd arrived there for a similar yet unrelated purpose, watching all of the action as it unfolded. He did not know them, and they were unaware of his presence.

Without hesitation, the driver and his accomplice yanked the men from the SUV, moved through the darkness and shoved them into the backyard of the desolate house. Strewn about the gargantuan yard was garbage, chunks of concrete and construction debris. They walked up the frail wooden steps and filed inside, smelling the room's putrid and disgusting odor, the kind that would have emanated from a rotting corpse. The four were thrust down into chairs, into pitch-black darkness as chatter from a nearby police scanner bellowed into the airspace.

Then, one of the captors turned on a table lamp, walked to a corner of the room, grabbed an AR-15 assault rifle with attached suppressor and racked the charging handle. The captured men shuddered and flailed at the sound of the lethal weapon engaging, and at what was sure to come next. Their breathing accelerated, their hearts pounding like the sound of bass marching drums. Their pulses hammered.

The man holding the rifle smirked as he walked toward them. He snatched the pouch from his nearest victim's head and viciously tore the tape from his mouth. He furrowed his brow. His forehead creased. "Do you know why you're here?" he asked.

The seated man gasped. His eyes bulged from their sockets in fear, welling up with tears. "Please don't do this," he spat out. "Listen. You got it all wrong, man. I swear. We can get you your money. A little more time is all we need. Please! *Please!*"

"I'm afraid it's too late for that."

The victim swiveled his neck toward the nearest window and shrieked: "Help! *Please, somebody help us!*" he called as loud as he could before breaking out into an uncontrollable sob.

"Shhhh... stop your whimpering. It's pathetic," the captor snapped. "I'm not going to shoot you. But you're all going to die a different way," he said as he forcefully taped the man's mouth again, covered his head with the black bag, and bound the drawstring tightly.

Moments later, the madman loomed over them, now holding a ten-inch hunting knife. Still seated, the men squirmed and writhed in fear, hands tied behind their backs and heads sheathed with those terrifying pouches, like the kind terrorists always used on their captives. The maniac then heaved a deep breath, moved closer to his nearest seated victim, and sliced into him, drawing the blade across his neck with the precision of a New York butcher. Suddenly, there was a violent ripping noise and a flaring sheet of agony. A euphoric rush surged from the inner depths of his consciousness as the killer maniacally decapitated the first of these four helpless souls.

The killer then nestled the knife against the dead man's cargo pants, and craned his neck toward the sound of approaching footsteps in the hall. There was a silhouette of a man lingering in the dimly lit doorway. One of the killer's cohorts walked into the room with an ominous warning.

"We got a problem."

CHAPTER 1

THE RIM OF DARKNESS

I WAS CHECKING my email when Max hurried over to me, wanting to go into the backyard. I closed my laptop, got up, and started toward the kitchen, when suddenly, I heard a strange sound from outside. It sounded like a person screaming for help. Max and I quickly went to open the backdoor to figure out from where the screams had emerged. But the doorbell suddenly rang, temporarily distracting me from investigating any further. I darted to the front door, peered out the peephole and opened it. Standing on my doorstep was an innocent-looking teenager with shoulder-length hair and an earring in his left ear, dressed like an Abercrombie and Fitch model.

"Hi, ma'am. We hate to bother you, but our car broke down by the corner, and we were wondering if you could call a tow truck for us. I left my cell at home, and my girlfriend's phone isn't charged."

"Sure, I guess I can do that. Hold on, let me grab mine and find one for you."

I used my phone's voice activation feature to contact a local towing company, then handed it to the teen to finish the call.

"Thanks so much, ma'am. My name is Aaron, by the way. My girlfriend and I will be in my car waiting. That's it by the curb. The black Camaro."

"That's a nice car. And you're welcome; let me know if you guys need anything else. I'll be home."

I stood on the porch as the boy returned to the car, got in and rolled down the windows. He and his girlfriend waited patiently, staring at the house next door as I watched and listened with rabid curiosity.

"Fuck—that is one creepy-looking place. And it's so huge. I just thought of a cool-ass idea, though. We could put out the word on Facebook we're having a party in there. Drinks, weed, sex—all for free. That would be totally awesome!" he said.

"Yeah, real smart, dipshit. Like anyone's going to go inside that disgusting house. So how long is it going to take the tow truck to come? And where is that asshole who's supposed to meet us here?" said the girl.

"The towing guy said maybe forty-five minutes to an hour. I think they're the only game in town. So calm down already, and quit freakin' out, all right?" the boy said sharply.

After I finished eavesdropping and closed the door, I hurled down the phone and hurried into the backyard, nervously seeking Max. I glanced at the chain-link fences on each side of the yard, and the old patio set in the middle that had been left by the previous owners. Then I glanced at the house next door, which was not only vacant, but was awaiting demolition or renovation, I'd been told. All the windows except for one were covered with wooden boards to prevent trespassers from entering. I yelled Max's name and, while looking in the direction of the house, suddenly saw a frenzied, jerky movement, behind the rear window. A strange figure stood there.

"What the hell?" I murmured.

I spun, Max came running and we both ran into the kitchen. I quickly closed the door and stared at the house through the miniblinds in my rear window. Was it a vandal? A thief? Even with being born and raised in Madison, the second largest city in Wisconsin, had not prepared me for whatever the hell could be happening here.

My heart accelerating rapidly, I grabbed my phone and dialed 911.

"911, what's your emergency?" queried the dispatcher on the other end.

"Yes, I want to report that someone is in the vacant house next door to me. I'm at 152 Mulholland Drive."

"Do you see anyone?"

"Yes, I saw some type of movement—and heard a scream. I believe someone is being attacked inside," I said nervously.

"Okay, ma'am, we'll send a patrol unit out right away. For your own safety, *please stay inside* your home and lock all doors," the dispatcher warned.

"Thank you." I glanced out the window a second time as I waited for the police to come. Suddenly, I saw two men bolt from the rear of the property, jack-knife over the chain-linked fence and leap into a waiting van that raged off, screeching around the corner. Several minutes later, there was the electronic squawk of sirens as the police arrived, guns drawn and flashlights in hand as they scoured the premises. A lone officer walked across the lawn, knocking on my door. I darted to the living room and opened it.

"Hi, my name is Crowley... Officer Mike Crowley. You called about suspicious activity next door?" he said. Crowley looked to be forty-something, and stood about six feet two, with an average build, dark curly hair, a five-o'clock shadow, a square chin, and under his sleeve, a distinctive tattoo on his right wrist with the initials E.S. inside of a pyramid.

"Yes, I did. I witnessed what looked like someone doing something strange in there. And then I saw two men fleeing the house after I finished the 911 call."

"We've searched around the premises, checked the bushes across the street, and glanced inside, didn't find anything. In that car sitting there are a couple of teenagers waiting for some assistance. Sometimes vacant houses become breeding grounds for all sorts of illegal activity, squatters, and even teenagers looking to get laid. I can understand your concern. You live here alone?"

"Yes, I do for now," I said, bewildered at where the conversation was heading.

"You haven't told me your name."

"I'm sorry, Alexis Fields. Pleased to formally meet you," I replied as I extended my hand to shake his.

"Are you new to the area? What do you do for a living?" he asked.

"I've recently relocated from Wisconsin, here for a new gig as an intern over at Veteran's Legacy Memorial."

"Well, at least you're not too far from home."

"It was a once-in-a-lifetime opportunity, so I couldn't pass it by."

"Congratulations, and I want to take this opportunity to officially welcome you to Lake Park. We've got a lot of people moving here. And I *hope and pray* we'll be able to keep out the bad element. Being close to Chicago has its advantages but, with all the crime they're experiencing, disadvantages, too. There's been an uptick in crime here, unfortunately, and everywhere else in the country, for that matter. It's the kind of world we live in now. It sucks; I know. The people that used to live in your house tried to start a neighborhood watch program before they left. But it never really got off the ground. Let us know if you see anything else, we're here to help," he said as his eyes traveled from my face down my body, and back up again before he turned to walk away.

"Okay, Officer. I will," I said. As I closed the door, I dully wondered if I had made the right move. I'd purchased my house as a short sale, and its close proximity to my job made the move to Lake Park an appealing choice. Crime was everywhere, I'd figured, but I'd only been living here a little over a week and already had to call the police regarding something suspicious next door. And then there was still the issue of Wilfred Bachman, my stalker ex-boyfriend I left behind.

Suddenly, my cell rang from across the room.

"Hello," I answered anxiously.

"Hi, there, girlfriend," said Carol, my longtime best friend from Madison.

"Carol, I'm glad you called!"

"What's going on? Is everything okay?"

"I just finished calling the police. There's something crazy going on at the vacant house next door to me. I let Max out in the yard and saw what looked like someone being assaulted over there through a window! The police just left."

"Really?" Carol said. "You know, I tell you Alexis, the world is a *very* scary place right now—no matter where you live. You *really* ought to buy a gun, like yesterday."

"I'll think about it. You know I don't like guns."

"I know. I know. But a girl's got to protect herself," said Carol.

"On a related note, I heard that your ex got into some kind of trouble. I'm not exactly sure what happened, but he seems to have totally lost it ever since you ended the relationship," Carol said.

"I haven't heard about it. Not that I really care, anyway."

"Well, things are moving along for you. And you've outwitted that creep of a man, Wilfred. You can now officially delete him from your memory."

"It's still an adjustment, moving to a new city and all, especially without any friends or family here. And of course, this is my first time being away from home. I really wish I had gone away to college. You'll have to come and visit soon. I've got room to spare," I said.

"I will. Just let me know when you have some days off. I'll come visit and we'll have a blast—margaritas, our *Turn It Up* contest, the whole nine. Drinks on me!"

"Well, I have to get up early. There's a staff meeting in the morning. I'm turning in and will talk to you by the weekend."

"Okay, girlfriend, and do me a favor, be safe," Carol said.

"I will. Bye."

I ended the call, ambled to my bedroom, set the alarm clock and flipped off the lights. After a few minutes, I had just drifted off when Max's frantic barking awoke me. I rose and went downstairs to settle him down, when suddenly; I heard some strange voices that appeared to be coming from *inside* the house. My heart pounding, I made a beeline for the kitchen and retrieved a knife from a nearby drawer. Slowly and nervously I tiptoed from room to room, my breathing becoming irregular, like a badly tuned, misfiring engine, as I heard what sounded like someone or something faintly whimpering.

"Who's there? I can hear you," I said. The voices seemed to become louder in the distance. It faintly sounded like someone asking for help… "*Help us*," I heard again.

While frantically looking for my phone to call 911, I grabbed a flashlight from a nearby closet. Both Max and I went to the basement door to further investigate. Slowly, I walked down the creaky steps, scanning the cold, dark room as Max stayed behind in fear at the top of the stairs. The flashlight quickly illuminated the unfinished basement full of clothes, miscellaneous boxes and extra furniture I'd brought with me from Wisconsin. As I crept forward, keeping my eyes straight ahead, I tripped over an aerobic step platform on the floor, tumbling down and slicing my knee with the knife as I attempted to break my fall. Mysteriously, the voices seemed to stop, as if I'd suddenly found where they'd originated.

Slowly, I hobbled back upstairs; Max began barking again. Happy to see me emerge from the basement, he wagged his tail and dashed across the room, barking at the front door.

"Max, *what* is the problem? You're not going out anymore tonight," I scowled, and talked him into settling down before peering out of the peephole. The voices started again. This time the source was clear. It was those goofy teens in the Chevy Camaro, curbside, in front of the house, chuckling and horsing around. Apparently, the tow truck had never arrived, and the driver, Aaron, got out to tighten some type of cable attached to the car's battery before climbing back in the driver's seat to crank the engine again.

On the other side of the car, there was a creepy-looking, disheveled, wide-eyed man, dressed in olive-colored khaki pants and a navy-blue hoodie, staring blankly at the teens from in between the bushes, watching, *riveted*. His face was weathered and his skin pallid against the dark backdrop of the nocturnal landscape. *Had the weirdo expected to see some amateur porn or something? Possibly—participate?*

They noticed him standing there. Their eyes traveled over him, terror-ridden in fear. The girl gasped from the passenger seat and screamed: "*Come on, start the car already, dammit!*"

Several minutes later, after numerous failed attempts to turn the engine, it finally started. The driver, dropping the accelerator, gripped the steering wheel and gunned it down Mulholland—leaving behind a plume of smoke.

It was no mystery why the teens had left in such a heart-wrenching panic. And who could blame them? Because there's one thing I suddenly knew for certain.

My life just became a whole lot scarier.

CHAPTER 2

THE FOLLOWING DAY at work was anything but normal. There'd been an anonymous bomb threat called into one of the nurses' stations. The caller alleged to have dynamite strategically placed in several of the hospital's wards as well as the trauma center and burn unit. Hospital security alerted the police and FBI. From outside of the front entrance, I watched nervously as they conducted a full-scale sweep of the premises. Eventually, it was determined that no actual explosives had been planted. Fortunately, most of my coworkers, and many patients, had been evacuated as a precaution until the search was completed.

Undaunted by the day's activities, I remained committed to making this opportunity work. It was my goal and my mother's that I'd become a doctor one day. Considerable amounts of time and money had already been invested in my future. After a long day that had seen an increase in emergency room activity, I went home. Both emotionally and physically drained now, all I could imagine was warming up one of my favorite leftover meals from yesterday (pappardelle with bolognese sauce) and taking a hot bath.

As I walked through the lobby area to exit the building, Kristal Andrews, a nursing attendant I'd met previously at one of the hospital's staff meetings, blurted that a particular doctor inquired about me.

"Thanks. However, if he's married, I'll pass. I just don't have time for drama. So who is the mystery man anyway?" I asked, stopping momentarily to hear the response.

"It's Dr. Khan, and yes, he is married. Still, I would be totally flattered."

"Is that so? And why do you say that, other than the fact that he's a doctor?"

Andrews smiled. "Most of the women who work here think he's good-looking, *and* he's working his way up. Word is, he's about to get a large research grant for some clandestine project he's been working on."

I shrugged, my curiosity piqued. "Doing what, exactly?"

"I don't know many details, other than it's dealing with new technology and medical devices. From what I understand, he'll be leaving the ER to work on it exclusively. And it's no secret around here that a lot of ER doctors eventually burn out, so I can see why he'd want to leave."

"Well, it all sounds really interesting, and I appreciate the attention, but I don't consider married men fair game. *And* he's a little out of my age range. Sorry, call me a prude if you will, but man sharing's not my thing," I replied, smiling. I then headed through the sliding glass doors and walked over to the employee parking lot.

Comfortably settling in my SUV, a silver metallic BMW X5 with a sunroof top and Harman Kardon sound system, I popped in Radiohead's *Pablo Honey* CD and weaved through the snarling traffic for the five-block trek to get home. As I pulled in front of my house and walked to the front door, I noticed a scribbled note on a yellow Post-it. *Stopped by just to check on you. C.* I'd had no idea who left the note, or who would have signed it with only the letter *C.* It was dark and after 8 p.m. now. Another tumultuous day in my life had faded into night, I thought pensively, and inserted my key in the door to go inside.

Max ran toward me, brushing against my leg and wagging his tail. I quickly trudged to the back door, letting him frolic in the backyard for several minutes. He'd never been fond of the doggy protection pad left in the kitchen for him while he was home alone.

After escorting him into the yard, I quickly realized I hadn't spoken to my mother in a week, and wanted to let her know that her "little girl" was okay. But before I had a chance to call, the doorbell rang. It was Mike Crowley, the presumptuous cop who had interviewed me when I'd called the police the day before. I opened the door.

"Hi, there. I stopped by earlier. I was the one who left the little sticky note. Just checking to see if you were okay. May I come in?" he asked.

"Sure."

"We're keeping a watch on the area just in case whoever was over at the house next door comes back. Have you seen anything else, Ms. Fields?"

"No, not since yesterday. I was actually hoping that someone would *buy* that damn house so it wouldn't be vacant!"

"I'll tell you this much, and I really didn't want to alarm you when we talked yesterday, but this area is *rapidly* changing, and it can be dangerous for a single woman like yourself not having some form of protection. I presume there's no man around." Crowley said and smirked. I was flabbergasted by his forwardness.

"You *are* single, aren't you, Ms. Fields?"

"Yes. Yes, I am," I said reluctantly.

"Well, why don't we get to know each other, hang out a little, do dinner? It'll be my treat. There are some nice places in town, and you know what they say about all work and no play." At that moment, he leaned over to whisper in my ear. "It makes for a boring existence," he said.

"Um, I don't think that would be such a good idea. I'm pretty much focused on work right now, don't really have the time," I said.

It didn't look like this cop was used to rejection; he seemed bewildered, his pale skin suddenly blushing red. "I'll give you some time to think about it," he replied with a coy wink.

"Okay, will do." I let Crowley out the front door and headed to the kitchen to heat up my leftovers. By the time I finished eating it was too late to call my mother, who was not much of a night owl. Instead, I decided to watch some TV before going to bed.

Most of the local news coverage was fixated on the bomb threat that had occurred earlier at Veteran's Memorial. The reporter was announcing that new details had emerged. My heart went into overdrive when a cop stated that a suspicious-looking man was seen peering into various entrances and exits of the hospital. Apparently, the only reason the scumbag didn't go inside was because a nearby pedestrian had reported the man to hospital security. The creep had then fled in a silver SUV. Reporters from various news stations were interviewing several staff members. Among those interviewed was Dr. K.M. Khan, the emergency room doctor I had been told about earlier.

The first thing I wondered was if it was Wilfred. He could have somehow followed me here to continue his sick campaign of harassment. After grabbing a cup of Chamomile tea to calm my nerves, I prepared my itinerary for work, took a shower, slipped into a silk nightgown and went to bed.

After lying asleep for several hours, I was suddenly jarred awake by shattering screams coming from outside. It sounded as if the screams were coming from the vacant house. I presumed it could have been those goofball teens again. I jerked out of bed, hurried downstairs, and flicked on the kitchen light. I then rushed to look out the back window, only to see a startlingly muscular man *peering back at me* from the other side of the fence next door. Bleary-eyed and in a hair-raising pulse of terror, I darted to the living room to get my house phone to call 911, but there was no dial tone. Panicking, I hurried across the room to retrieve my iPhone from my purse. The battery was down, with not enough of a charge to make the call.

"Dammit!" I shrieked loudly.

I sprinted to the front window and watched through the blinds as a group of men hustled from the side to the front of the house. My heart began racing, and I could hardly credit what I was seeing. One of the men *looked like* Mike Crowley, the cop that had come to my door earlier, but I wasn't sure it was him. Impulsively, I opened the front door and yelled: "Mike Crowley?"

"I'll be right there," the man replied. I could vaguely see his face, and what looked like a badge bristling and reflecting against the glare of the streetlights. Whatever had occurred, I felt somewhat at ease knowing that the police were next door looking into the matter. Meanwhile, Max darted to the door in an attempt to go outside. I watched as the men put a large bag into a waiting van, then rushed toward my house.

As the men approached, I bluntly asked: "What's going on? It sounded like I heard someone scream over there." At that time, as they drew closer and their pace faster, all four, including Crowley, barreled through the front door, ambushed me, pummeled and kicked me while shoving me to the ground. I kicked and screamed as the four of them struggled to bind my hands, feet and mouth with duct tape. My dog, Max, now in full attack mode, barked frantically, attacking the men and biting their legs, his teeth puncturing their skin to the point of drawing blood. The men howled and kicked as they tussled with both Max and me. Then, Mike Crowley, struggling to control the situation with one hand, withdrew a large black handgun with the other and shot my dog. Max screamed in pain and horror and collapsed on the carpet. As these scumbags continued to hold me, I watched as Max lay there, bleeding, choking out his last desperate breath, still writhing in pain.

Frantically, I fought, kicked and tried with every ounce of my soul to squirm away. They lifted me and carried me out the back door, through the yard and over to the vacant house. The four of them shuffled up an old wooden porch, struggling, still grasping my body, then opened the back entrance to the property, carried me inside and dropped me onto the cold wooden floor.

"You're going to learn to shut the fuck up. Everything was fine until *you* moved here," Crowley said. Then he knelt, closing in on my face, peering at me with malevolent eyes. "You want to see what's going on? Tonight you get something to talk about," he said as the rest of the men chuckled. "Hold her down," Crowley blurted, trying to catch a breath as he motioned to several of the other cops to grab my arms and feet. The rest of them watched as Crowley sexually assaulted me. Two of them held me down while another videotaped the whole ordeal on his cell phone, laughing while narrating the assault like it was some sort of sick sporting event. Semiconscious, I scanned the space, which appeared to be a den, and tried to make sense of what was happening. The house reeked with the odor of death and evil from all the atrocities that had obviously taken place here. They continued to beat me and left me on the floor, bruised and in pain. As I lay on the floor, barely able to breathe, the sons of bitches prepared to leave the room to head toward the basement.

"Now we've got a problem on our hands," said one of the men.

"What do you want to do with her?" asked another.

"Let's move the rest of this shit to the van in case there are more nosy fucking neighbors, and when we're done, finish her off," Crowley said boisterously.

I watched them through my peripheral vision and the narrow slits of my lids. I convincingly played either totally unconscious or dead. Be still. Don't breathe. *Don't fucking breathe!* I told myself, desperate to survive. As soon as they left my sight, I pulled myself together through sheer will and determination and managed the strength to sit upright, then crawled to the only window in the room. I rose, getting my feet beneath me, barely able to stand, I pushed the old rusty lever to one side, unlocking the window. And with the only reserve of strength I had left, raised the window high enough to escape. The frame made a high-pitched squealing sound as I lifted it. Suddenly, as I hefted one leg up to climb out, I could hear Crowley and his cohorts laughing and heading back toward the room. Their voices were getting louder. I took a deep breath, looking down onto the dark terrain of the street, and jumped. As my feet pounded the ground with a painful *THWAP*, I could hear the assholes shouting in a fit of rage as they returned to the room.

"Where'd she go?" one of them asked.

"Find that bitch *now!*" another barked.

As I hobbled across the street, hiding between several parked cars, I watched as they searched the grounds, then rushed over to my house to see if I'd gone there. They had no clue I was close by, hiding in plain sight. After searching to no avail, they jumped in a black SUV and canvassed the neighborhood to find me.

After hiding in the bushes and between parked cars on Mulholland to elude them, I was able to hobble five blocks to the hospital where I worked. Once inside, I collapsed on my way to the emergency room. The frightening glimpse and reflection in the ER's sliding glass doors revealed that the side of my face was red and swollen, my royal blue nightgown torn and bloodied.

"Alexis... what happened to you? Oh my God," yelled one of nurse practitioners who had recognized me. Several other nurses on duty quickly came to my aid, along with a nursing assistant.

"I was attacked and raped!" I said, crying and shaking hysterically.

Hospital staff swiftly ushered me in for treatment, whisking me into the emergency room for observation. Fifteen seconds later, Dr. K.M. Khan, the ER doctor on duty, came into the room.

"Ms. Fields, I'm so sorry that this has happened to you, and recognize you as one of our own here," he said, as the team prepared to examine me and administer a rape kit. How ironic was it that Khan was the doctor who had been inquiring about me, wanting to get acquainted on a personal level, even though he was married? I thought.

"We'll do everything we can for you. Have the police been notified?" Khan asked.

"No," I replied dully.

"I will have the police alerted right away then," he said in some foreign accent.

"No, wait. At least one of the men involved was a police officer," I said.

"What?" said Khan, seemingly baffled. "Are you certain?"

"Yes, I'm sure."

"I have contacts within Lake Park PD. We'll get to the bottom of this so that those who are responsible for hurting you are brought to justice, immediately. I'll be right back." The emergency room nurses continued to administer to me, while Khan walked across the hall.

He returned several minutes later with cell phone in hand. "I became friends with a cop who investigated when my Escalade was stolen from the hospital's employee parking lot, and bonded with him further after he was seriously hurt in an off-duty car accident," he explained. He pressed the Speaker button on his smartphone for me to hear the conversation. I tried to listen while concentrating on what the nurses were doing to my body.

"Hello, my friend. It's Dr. Khan, how are you?"

"Good, good. Things are looking up, what more can we mortals ask for?"

"Listen, I wish I was calling on more favorable terms, but I have a victim here who is also one of our interns. She wants to report being beaten and sexually assaulted. However, she said that one of the perpetrators involved was a police officer. And so that's why I wanted to contact you first."

"Are you serious?"

"Yes, unfortunately."

"What's her name?"

"Alexis Fields. She moved to the area about a week ago."

"You think she's telling the truth, or delusional, maybe?"

"I believe her, plus we're administering a rape kit now, so that will tell us something for sure."

"Okay, we'll have someone over to take a report. Don't worry; she'll be looked after. I'll see to it personally."

After being treated by the doctor and the nursing staff and given a new set of clothing, I waited to be interviewed by the responding officer regarding the attack. Meanwhile, one of the nurses who had recognized me was kind enough to give me a pay-as-you-go cell phone, which she had purchased earlier in the day for her son. After listening to the cop on the phone, I was hoping they'd send someone with a modicum of compassion, who could also be impartial.

A half hour later, the responding officer arrived at the hospital, paperwork in hand and food stains on his shirt, as if he had just eaten. I stared at the short, overweight man with his protruding paunch and full head of white hair as he approached. Apparently, he had been given my exact description and where I could be found waiting. He had an expression on his face that was somewhere between bored and annoyed, like this was the kind of interview he'd done a million times throughout his career.

"Ms. Fields, Roger Hallahan, Lake Park PD. I understand you were sexually assaulted and beaten?" he asked, while preparing to jot down notes on his clipboard.

"Yes, that's correct," I said.

"I'm sorry to hear that. Looks like another feather in the cap for Second Amendment Rights. I'll be taking a report on the incident. Any description of your attackers?"

"Yes, and I want to mention that one of them was a police officer."

"And how do you know *that*?" he replied, almost combatively.

"Because... I met him previously when I called about suspicious activity next door to my home, his name is Mike Crowley."

"Mike Crowley? He's one of our most popular and well-liked officers, and part of the Special Operations Section. Are you sure you're not mistaken?" he asked.

"Yes, I'm certain."

"Okay, as a formality, I'll need for you to come down to the station for an in-depth interview. Can you come now? If you're not up to it this evening, I completely understand, and we'll just reschedule for another day," the cop said.

"Sure, I'll come now—because I want the son of a bitch punished!" I snapped.

The cop and I left the hospital, walked across the street to a parked cruiser and got in. But he hesitated once in the driver's seat.

"Aren't you going to start the car?" I quipped.

"Not until I talk to you first, bitch!" barked a threatening growl from the backseat.

I froze, horrified, and was starting to hyperventilate, as I suddenly recalled that terrifying voice. Slowly, I craned my neck around to look. It could have only been Mike Crowley hiding in that backseat.

And it was.

Crowley scowled: "You need to let this go—no, actually, you need to move back to whatever rock you crawled out from under, because you're in way over your head. This thing is much bigger than me, and you're interfering with the wrong people's money. If you continue to make waves, you will be buried in steel containers like the rest of the assholes that got in my way, and your family will never find you. Now... you can go to the station and *hope* that someone believes you, *or,* you can pack your shit and leave town now! It's that simple. You've been warned!"

Trembling and confused, I exited the police cruiser and started walking as fast as I could, back toward the hospital. I walked past the entrance to the ER, with no idea who to trust, or where I would go from here.

"Ms. Fields," a man suddenly called as he approached from inside the hospital foyer.

"My name is John Hill; I'm with the hospital's crisis management team. I received information about what happened to you, and I'm here to help any way that I can. Do you have a ride home?"

"I can't go back there; it's not safe anymore."

"Well, unless you have somewhere else to go, there's a nice hotel near downtown, the Radisson Plaza. How about I give you a ride there?" he said.

"Um, not so sure about that. I need to see some identification first. I need to know you are who you say you are."

"Sure," he replied as he went into his wallet to retrieve a photo ID. "I don't blame you one bit."

I looked at the photo, then up at his face. "Thank you," I said.

We climbed in his SUV and continued to talk as he started the engine.

"I've read the report, and I know what you've been through. I'll be here to help you every step of the way. This is going to be an uphill battle. We're going to need all the evidence that we can get our hands on. This is no ordinary circumstance."

"I have this," I muttered, as I held up a small black address book.

"I took it from the front seat of the squad car I was in. I think it belongs to Crowley," I said.

"Is that the man who attacked you?"

"Yeah, he and three others, but mainly him."

"Can I see that?" Hill asked, as he maneuvered the SUV with one hand while looking at the address book with the other.

"I recognize some of these names. There are some very powerful people in here. Be prepared. They're going to come after you," he said as he handed me back the book.

Shortly after midnight, we arrived at the hotel and I checked myself into a room. I deemed it necessary to wait until morning to call my family and my best friend Carol to tell them what happened. And no matter how much I wanted to, or how tired I became, I could not fall asleep. Still on edge, I decided to tread over to the hotel's business center to log on to the Internet, trying to process how my life had just been changed forever.

I searched online to learn more about Lake Park, the community where I'd purchased my home, and for anything I could discover about Crowley. "Un-frigging-believable!" I muttered, and was flabbergasted to see so many articles and civilian complaints about him and Lake Park PD. I filtered through additional pages of Google search results, then clicked on an interesting link which read:

LAKE PARK COP ACQUITTED OF MURDER

This was the most heart-wrenching article; it told how he'd been implicated in the murder of a young coed who had lived off campus at nearby Forestville University. He had been acquitted due to uncooperative witnesses and a lack of evidence. Although, according to the article, it was common knowledge around Lake Park that he'd had some type of personal relationship with her.

I searched through additional pages and read detailed complaints the police department had received concerning Crowley—everything from sexual harassment to police brutality. Still, through it all, how in hell had he managed to remain a cop? I wondered. I sighed and took a deep breath, believing with all my heart that something needed to be done. Widespread corruption had obviously taken over Lake Park, just as it had so many other cities. This was the only way that Crowley could remain untouched, I thought.

CHAPTER **3**

THE STRESS AND anxiety of the day eventually took their toll, causing me to fall asleep in the chair in the hotel's business center. The following morning I contacted the managerial staff at the hospital to arrange for more time off and to leave my new contact information.

Later that day I was contacted by Internal Affairs Division (IAD) investigators requesting an interview. I obliged. However, when the investigators arrived, they were anything but sympathetic.

"Ms. Fields?" one of the men said after arriving. "I'm Will McDermott, and this is my partner Ed Bradstone from IAD of the Lake Park PD. We would like to talk to you about the incident reported and your accusations against one of our officers. May we come in?"

"Sure," I said.

"Now, you mind telling us what happened?" McDermott asked.

I began explaining in detail the night of the attack as it unfolded, sobbing as I talked and wiping falling tears from my cheeks. Both investigators look bewildered, interrupting me abruptly.

"Ma'am, with all due respect, the statement that we've obtained from the officer involved strongly contradicts your statements concerning what happened that night. His version of accounts was that the two of you were involved in a casual relationship, had consensual sex, and subsequently, you went ballistic when he told you that he wasn't interested in anything serious. He then stated that the two of you got into a physical altercation, at which time, he had to defend himself against you and your dog—which also attacked him."

"That's bullshit, a fucking lie! Everything I've told you is the truth. The man is a disgrace to the police department and a monster." Suddenly, there was utter silence in the room.

My eyes slowly angled toward the floor. Feeling dejected, I said, "I don't know who to trust anymore. I don't know why I'm talking to you without a lawyer. All I have is my faith to lean on now."

Throughout the interview, I'd noticed that McDermott and Bradstone were cautious never to use Crowley's name. They both concluded their questions and thanked me for my time.

"We'll be in touch. Here's my card, if you think of anything else," McDermott said as they left the room.

I suddenly realized that I had not called my mother or best friend Carol, the two people who mattered most in my life. I had no siblings, and my father and I had been estranged most of my life after my parents divorced.

Sitting alone in the room, I reflected again on the decision to accept the internship at the hospital, and pondered whether my life was in a downward spiral. It was evident now that the move to Lake Park and the new career opportunity had been anything but ideal.

I composed myself and found the courage to pick up the phone and call my mother.

"Mom, it's me," I said.

"Alexis, I've been trying to reach you. I've left several messages for you and got worried when I didn't hear back from you. Are you okay?" my mother asked.

I hesitated. "Uh, no, Mom, I'm not okay," I said, my voice starting to quiver. "I was raped and beaten."

"Oh my God," my mother said, sounding shaken as she too started to cry. "Alexis, what happened?"

"I saw some suspicious people outside, next door, and thought I recognized one of the men as a police officer I met previously after I called 911. When I yelled his name, he and several others busted through my door and attacked me. They also shot and killed Max, Mom."

"You need to come home now! It's not safe for you there living alone. Come back home. I'll help you! Have the people responsible for this been caught?"

"No, Mom, as I said, this guy is one of them. This city and police department are so corrupt. This is much bigger than what it seems, and that's why I'm going to stay and fight. If no one stands up to them, nothing is going to change. I have to do this!"

"Oh God, Alexis, I'm so worried about you."

"Mom, I promise—I'll be okay."

"Look, I'm coming there to be with you. You should not be alone, and I'm not taking no for an answer."

"Mom, let me handle this my way. Besides, you may be in grave danger if you come here. I'll keep you posted, I promise."

"I'm not taking no for an answer, Alexis!"

"Hold on, Mom, I have another call coming in," I said as I clicked over to take the call.

"Alexis, this is John Hill. I've uncovered some new information; we need to talk as soon as possible. Can we meet today?"

"Sure, how about in an hour?"

"Okay, that works for me. I'll swing by the hotel to pick you up."

"Alright, I'll be ready."

"Hello, Mom. That was John Hill on the other line, a helpful guy I met from the hospital's crisis management team. He told me he had some new information and he wants to meet with me. He said he wants to help me with my case, and I'll be seeing him in an hour. I'll give you a call later and keep you posted."

"Alexis, please call me soon and let me know that you're okay."

"I will. Love you, bye."

After talking to my mother, I prepared for the meeting with John Hill. Barely presentable, I showered and pinned back my hair, forced to wear the same hospital-supplied clothes I'd been given the day before.

CHAPTER **4**

MY MOTHER, DORIS FIELDS, was not one to stand by idly, and Carol informed me that her brother, Jason, had recently seen my mother at the United Airlines ticket counter at Dane County Regional Airport. After I finished talking to Carol about my harrowing ordeal, I got dressed and prepared to leave.

Minutes later, John Hill arrived in the Radisson's parking lot, entered the front lobby and used his cell phone to call my room, for me to come down for our impromptu meeting at a local breakfast cafe. He was adamant about personally walking me to the parking lot to ensure my safety.

"Alexis, good to see you again," he said as he watched me exit the elevator.

Sheepishly, I shook Hill's hand while surveying the guests waiting to check in at the reservations desk. We both exited the lobby, passing weary travelers resting comfortably on gray modular furniture, and headed toward the parking lot.

During our conversation as we rode through the morning traffic, I learned more about Hill and felt at ease in his presence. He seemed a good-natured man with a laidback personality. He had a good education, which included two master's degrees, and had never been married, he told me.

We slowly pulled up in front of Morrissey's, the cute little diner that was a favorite among Lake Park residents for its excellent food and ample portions. Hill opened the door to the restaurant, and we were immediately greeted by a hostess.

"We'd like a table for two," he said.

"Sure, follow me. A booth okay?" the hostess asked.

"Perfect," Hill said, as we settled into a burgundy faux-leather booth, glancing over the menus placed on the table. He was eager to get started.

"Alexis, based on the information you've given me, I've done some more research and come up with additional information."

Before he could continue, we were both interrupted by a waitress asking to take our order.

"Hi, how are both of you? My name is Tracy, what can I get for you this morning?"

"I'll have coffee, cream and sugar, and the number three combo, eggs over easy."

"And you, ma'am?"

"I'll have a cup of hot tea and wheat toast, no butter. Sorry, I don't have much of an appetite this morning."

"That's quite okay. I'll have that right up for you," the waitress said.

Hill continued. "So, Alexis, I've been doing my research, and the more I look into this, the more interesting things become. I've searched city records and it appears that there has been an unusually large amount of construction going on in your area, particularly at the location where the vacant house is. Now it could all be just a coincidence, but I think there's more to it than meets the eye."

"So what exactly have you found?" I asked.

"Well, for starters, there's this construction company, Gene & Elle Construction, Inc., one of the largest construction firms in Lake Park. From what I gather, they only seem to get involved with large, commercial-type construction projects, so who in their right mind would hire them for construction on a single-family home in a residential neighborhood? Also, there's a previous report that linked Lake Park's city manager with the owners of Gene & Elle in some type of pay-to-play scheme. But the craziest thing of all is: despite the alleged ongoing construction, the condition of the house still remains the same, dilapidated and vacant."

"So, you're saying there's more to that house than what we can see?"

"It's certainly worth looking into, and *I* think we should go there—try to get in if possible and look around," Hill said.

"Are you crazy? If they catch us, not could they only arrest us for trespassing, they would also want to *kill us*," I said.

Hill beamed. "The way I look at it, you were attacked in that house and have every right to go back there to look for your personal belongings, if you know what I mean."

I shook my head. "Okay, so when do you propose we do this?"

"I've got a Handycam camcorder. The recording time is longer than what I'd get from my cell phone. I'll pick you up and we'll go over there tonight to get a closer look, to see exactly what's going on. *But only if you're up to it.*" Several minutes later, the waitress brought our food as we continued to talk.

"Here's a number three combo, coffee, a cup of hot tea, a side of wheat toast and no butter. Did I forget anything? Can I get either of you anything else?"

"No, we're good for now," Hill replied.

The waitress briefly scanned the room and said, "I wanted to mention to you both, there was a guy seated at the window over there. He asked me if you came here often. I didn't answer him because he looked so weird and creepy. I'd never seen him before."

"Well, we appreciate that. There are a lot of nutcases running around these days. If he comes back, please let us know," said Hill.

"I will. You both have a good day."

"Thanks, you do the same."

"You know, I haven't told anyone about this before today. But I've been experiencing the most excruciating pain in my left arm. Even now, it feels as if someone is poking me with an ice pick. How lucky I must be, huh?" I said.

"You think it's from the incident?"

"I'm not sure. That's what's so weird. It didn't start until I went to the ER that night, and it's been hurting like hell ever since."

"If I were you, I'd let your doctor know. It's probably nothing to worry about. At least get it checked out so you'll have peace of mind."

"You're right. I'll make an appointment and get an MRI scheduled. I *work* there, so you'd think I'd know better."

"I wonder what the folks that lived in your house before you experienced while there. You know much about the people who sold it to you?" Hill asked.

"Actually, it was a bank-owned property; the previous owners were in default and lost the house. I got a pretty good deal on it, so—"

"I bet you did. Isn't your address 152 Mulholland?"

"Yep, that's it."

"I've got an idea," Hill said.

"What's that?"

"I've got a good friend who's a realtor, Richard Akins. I'm going to see if he can find out more information about your house and the one next door." Hill pulled out his cell phone to send a text to his friend. "He's usually pretty quick with getting back to me. And he's got access to a ton of information."

The text read:

I wanted to ask a favor of you. I'm trying to get information on two properties in the area. The first is 152 Mulholland Drive, and the other is next door at 158 Mulholland. Anything you could find out about the previous owners, or what's going on with these homes, as far as any activity, would be most appreciated, my friend. Thanks, John Hill.

"Hold on, John, someone is calling me," I said as I pressed the Talk button on the cell phone I'd been given.

"Ms. Fields?"

"Yes, who's calling?"

"This is Lou Haney with Madison PD. How are you're doing?"

"Okay, I guess, could be better."

"Your mother was gracious enough to give me your new cell number. The reason for my call is because I wanted to give you a heads-up. Wilfred Bachman, your ex-boyfriend, or fiancé, has been eluding law enforcement for a while now, and his whereabouts are still unknown at this time. He's been in an unstable state of mind ever since what happened here, and I wanted to reach out to you as a courtesy to tell you to watch your back."

"Well, I appreciate you letting me know, and that's one of the reasons why I've since relocated. I couldn't stand the creep."

"I completely understand; it's best to take these types of things seriously. And so, that's why I wanted to call. That being said, you take care of yourself, Ms. Fields, and let me know if I can be of any help."

"I sure will. Thank you."

I glanced at Hill as he enabled the speaker on his cell and answered the call from his friend.

"Rich, I'm glad I could reach you quickly."

"Hey, John, you know me. Got to make myself available at all times. So here's what I was able to find. There was a Waldrop family that lived at 152 Mulholland until they disappeared last year, and the case has never been solved. Police assumed there was foul play involved. I remember this story, too, in the media; they never found a trace of 'em. Police weren't sure if it was an abduction, or a murder-suicide that may have occurred elsewhere. As for 158 Mulholland, the city is listed as the owner. And there isn't much info available on that one, which is kind of weird to say the least."

"Rich, back to the family that disappeared, how long ago was that?"

"It was in September of last year. The house was vacant for a while until it was sold to the current owner, which looks like an Alexis Fields. Hopefully, all of that was disclosed before the sale. Do you know this person?"

"She's a friend of mine I'm trying to help."

"I'll let you know if anything else comes up when I have more time to dig. I've got a showing in ten minutes. Hope this helps."

"I appreciate it, Rich. We'll catch up when you get some time."

"Okay, John, it's always easier to reach me via text or email. Talk to you soon," Akins said.

Hill ended the call and stared at me blankly.

"It baffles me how a family can just vanish, never to been seen or heard from again. More troubling is the fact that the authorities don't know if there was any foul play, or if the family just decided to up and walk away. I hate that you had to learn all of this after the fact, Alexis."

"Are you friggin kidding me? How come nobody told me this? I should have been told by *somebody* that this happened. Isn't there a law that says something like that has to be disclosed to a homebuyer?"

"According to my friend, it sounds like you should have been made aware, initially."

"Oh, I feel safe *now*. I get raped by a cop, my ex is nowhere to be found, and then I find out that a family may have been murdered in my house!"

"I know... I know... hopefully we can find some answers," Hill said.

"There's so much I have to do. I have to complete paperwork for more time off work. I have to get my belongings from the house, because I'm not going back there to live. Hopefully, I can find a reasonable hotel to live in for an extended length of time."

"I'm here for you; consider me a friend. We'll go over there tonight. My goal is to get as much evidence as we can—to blow this case wide open."

We both finished eating as Hill summoned the waitress before preparing to take me back to the Radisson.

"John, can I ask another favor? Would you mind taking me to my house while it's daylight, today? I really need to get some basic necessities for now, and my car. I feel much safer with you there with me."

"Sure, we can go now if you're ready. My treat today," he said. We left Morrissey's, entered Hill's SUV and drove to my house. Once we pulled in front I got out and walked to the front door, slowly turning the handle. To my surprise, the door was neither locked nor shut. Hill followed close behind.

Once inside, I gathered some of my belongings, the most important things that I'd need for my stay at the hotel. Hill looked around and noticed signs of the struggle. There was the knocked-over furniture and the broken vase that I'd purchased on a trip to Cancun, as well as dried bloodstains on the carpet.

"What happened here?" he asked.

"That's where those assholes shot and killed my dog, Max, and then lied about the whole thing," I said.

"I'm sorry to hear that. With those types of scumbags, nothing they do surprises me," he said. Hill continued to look around curiously and noticed the framed picture on the mantel. "Is that your mom?"

"Yeah, and she's worried to death about me."

"Well, I'll bet she's proud of you, the things that you've accomplished, especially at such a young age."

"She wanted to come here, but I told her it was too dangerous, and that she needed to stay home," I said as I gathered as many things as I could fit in a plastic bag to take back to the hotel, including my extra set of keys, iPhone and journal. "Okay, I'm ready. I can always return for more things as needed; this should hold me over for now," I said.

We both walked out of the house. I was sure to lock the door this time with my key. As I headed toward my BMW, and Hill toward his vehicle, a suspicious-looking SUV with tinted windows slowly crept by, rap music blaring, while the vehicle's occupants, sporting facial tattoos and sunglasses, stared menacingly at both Hill and me.

"Now *that* was creepy. You *know* those guys?" he asked.

"Nope, never seen them before, but I agree—they did look shady."

"Look, it's important that we're on the same page here, and stick together no matter what. We don't know what in the hell we're going to find in that house, so we have to be prepared for anything. We'll wait until it gets dark. I'll pick you up at nine thirty tonight," he said.

"Alright. Let's hurry up and get out of here. It's not safe," I said. We both got in our vehicles and headed back to the Radisson.

Traffic was tight as we approached downtown. It was a midday rush in the city, and we eventually pulled up to the front entrance of the hotel. After I exited my vehicle, I spun and said to Hill, "Thank you for being understanding and supportive, but most of all—thank you for your courage."

"You're welcome. This is something that's been a long time coming," he replied. I shuffled inside to put away my belongings and to reflect on what Hill and I were about to do.

I stared at the clock, nervously counting the hours as they went by. With each passing moment, it became more and more evident that we were putting ourselves in grave danger. At 9:25, my phone rang. It was Hill, calling to let me know that he was outside.

"I'll be right down," I said.

The moment I got in his SUV, the countdown began; we surmised that this undertaking could reveal more than either of us cared to admit. We nervously anticipated what lay ahead as we approached the hideous-looking house.

I exited the vehicle first, sheepishly looking around as Hill and I walked hurriedly to the side of the two-story dwelling, toward the backyard. The tall, barrier fence around most of the yard had been covered with some type of paper, apparently to prevent prying eyes from catching a glimpse of any nefarious activity.

One at a time, we climbed over the eight-foot-tall fence, and landed on the other side, hitting the ground with seemingly bone-shattering impact. Construction and excavation equipment was everywhere.

"Hey, here's an opening. This must be the back door. Looks like my time as a carpenter in the military is about to come in handy. One thing I can do is pry open a locked door," said Hill. As soon as he opened it, we were hit with the stench, the same disgusting odor that I'd smelled when I was assaulted here.

We entered what appeared to be a stairway to the main floor, but decided to go in the basement first. Hill quickly turned on his flashlight and Handycam. We held hands as we slowly plodded past the leaking plastered ceiling, the graffiti-covered walls, and the dead cockroaches. As we cautiously approached a larger room, we could faintly hear what sounded like cries for help further away. We quickly noticed that the size of the basement far exceeded what would normally be built for a house of such size.

We both looked around, hoping to draw closer to the wretched calls we'd heard. As we continued into the abysmal, near pitch-black darkness—still holding hands—Hill's Maglite started to flicker.

"*Dammit!* I think this thing's going out on me," he said. He hit the side of the flashlight with his fist, hoping it would help. It didn't. "I've still got the light on my Handycam. It's not as good, but it's better than nothing," he said. With less light to guide us now, our ability to see anything at a distance was severely diminished.

As we wandered aimlessly with no sense of direction, we stumbled upon a room. The stench that permeated the house became even more prominent as we got closer to the room's door. Slowly turning the knob, Hill entered first, and I followed close behind him, with a knot in my stomach and my heart pounding rapidly.

He held up his camcorder to illuminate and record what looked like wooden crates neatly stacked near the corner, three up and four across. As we inched closer, Hill laid his Handycam down so we could open the top container. Although we feared what might lurk inside, our curiosity got the best of us.

Once the lid was removed, Hill picked up his camcorder so we could peer inside. "Un-friggin-believable, it's enough weapons here to equip a small army," he whispered fiercely. "Inside are AK-47s, AR-15 assault rifles, grenades, and an assortment of handguns, including Glocks and nine-millimeter Berettas."

We opened more containers and found packages of what appeared to be heroin, cocaine and marijuana neatly packaged and ready for sale and distribution. Hill took pictures of each with his cell phone before we closed the crates and left the room.

Suddenly, we heard a nearby door open and slam shut. Voices of men talking could be heard. The sound of the voices became louder, proof the men were getting closer.

"Oh, shit, we've got to hide. Go back in the room. We'll hide behind the containers," Hill said. We hid in the room, and the voices of the men echoed in the hallway as they walked by.

As the coast cleared, we squeezed out of the small space behind the weapon-filled containers. Hardly able to see and trying to avoid being entangled in spider webs, I tripped over what appeared to be a large black duffel bag.

"What the hell is *that?*" I whispered. Hill opened the bag, and we both gasped at the grisly sight of four bloody severed heads inside. They were badly decomposing, and the gruesome discovery almost made us both puke on the spot. Hill quickly snapped a photo with his cell.

We tried our best to contain our emotions as we attempted to exit the room to escape. Not knowing what direction to go in, we were ultimately drawn toward the moans that we'd heard down the hall.

Quickly creeping through the dark corridor, we came upon another room. The pleas for help became louder as we approached the door. What could possibly be on the other side? I wondered in terror.

Hill slowly opened the door and what we saw sent chills down our spine. On the floor were women and girls, at least fourteen of them, gagged, chained, some apparently suffering from malnourishment and dehydration, all of them held in what appeared to be a dreadful holding room, suffering torturously as sex slaves, and some sort of amusement for their sadistic captors.

Tears welled in my eyes as Hill and I remained helpless from doing anything. Their eyes pleaded for mercy. We peered around for anything that could release them—a key, a tool, *anything*. But we knew, regrettably, there was nothing we could do right now but leave. Hill took out his cell phone for a photo, another that could undoubtedly help blow the lid off the case. The women and girls were chained to brackets on the wall specifically devised for enslavement.

After a quick exit, we came upon another door. Surprisingly, light leaked from underneath it. I grabbed the handle, slowly turning it so as to not make any noise while Hill readied his camcorder. Once it was open slightly, we both peeked through the gap. We were flabbergasted at the sight.

There were retractable stairs leading down to what looked like a small city underground, a high-tech criminal enterprise, complete with lights, a paved roadway, storage facilities and some kind of tunnel that led to God only knew where. There were parked cars, box trucks, forklifts, and men scurrying back and forth moving containers full of drugs and weapons.

"So *this* is what all the construction is about. They must still be adding more," I said.

Hill snapped a photo. "Let's go; we've got to keep moving," he said. We both retreated backwards, away from the door, walking at a fast pace, with Hill holding up his cell for light. The phone proved to be a good choice at this point with its ability to take wide panoramic pictures in the dark. But to our dismay, the phone's battery indicator started showing there wasn't much of a charge left.

We moved through the dark corridor, and as we approached what appeared to be a utility closet, we could hear squirming and muffled whimpering. We both grabbed the doorknob simultaneously and turned it. The door opened slowly.

"Oh my God!" I blurted, my heart racing rapidly. *It was my mother!* who had stubbornly come to help, but was abducted and being held captive by Crowley and his henchmen.

Hill and I were able to remove the duct tape to free her. There was no time for questions. We helped her from the closet and the three of us bolted down the corridor, praying that whatever was at the end would lead us to the outside world. My mother, struggling to keep up, fell, knocking over several shovels perched against a wall. Hearing the noise, Crowley's crew came running out of the meeting taking place down the hallway.

"Get those motherfuckers!" one yelled as they all raced toward us. The three of us then turned a corner and ran for our lives through the monstrous basement.

"Quick, there's a window," Hill said, as he moved to open the safety latch. The three of us climbed out as Crowley's men turned the corner, realizing that we had gotten away. Once outside, we ran toward Hill's SUV, still reeling from what had happened inside. Hill quickly fired up his vehicle and thundered off, burning tire marks in the street.

"Mom, what were you doing? I told you to stay home!" I turned and scolded, my voice shaking with anxiety. While we conversed, Hill looked out of his rearview to see if we were being followed.

"I couldn't stay home not knowing what's going on with you. I knew if I told you I was coming you'd try to talk me out of it. And when I was unable to find you at the Radisson, I caught a cab to your house, the only other place I knew to go looking."

Hill interjected, "Alexis, don't blame your mom. She did what most mothers would do. She loves you."

"What should we do next?" I asked.

"Well, we've got pictures, video, and concrete evidence that shows what's going on. I have a friend named Bruce Massey who works at Harbor Media Group. He's got tons of media contacts and I trust him. I say we go that route first since we can't go to the police."

Twenty minutes later, we approached the Radisson.

"I'll walk you guys up to the room," Hill said, while scanning the parking lot to see if the coast was clear. "I'll pick you guys up at ten a.m. We'll grab breakfast then visit my friend." The three of us walked into the hotel lobby and toward the first bank of elevators to go upstairs. "This has been some day. Ms. Fields, your daughter is a true fighter, and I'm with her every step of the way."

My mother turned her head sideways to respond. "She can be very stubborn at times, Mr. Hill." After reaching our floor we got off the elevator and walked down the hall.

Hill smiled. "Stay safe, ladies," he said as he turned from the door to go home. My mother and I thanked him and quickly rushed into the room, still discussing the day's events as we closed the door and secured the lock.

The next morning, Hill arrived at 10 sharp. We had breakfast at the Denny's restaurant around the corner before going to see his friend, whom he had already called to confirm the meeting.

Harbor Media Group was on the other side of town, located in a swank Art Deco commercial district. We arrived a few minutes before noon, curiously looking around as we marveled at the expensive-looking office foyer. The visitors' waiting area was surrounded by windows and featured a beautiful, rich, colorful décor—hand-painted abstract canvas art, contemporary furniture and an espresso-colored marble floor.

"Hi, we're here to see Bruce Massey, programming director," Hill said to the receptionist.

"Who should I say is here?"

"John Hill and my two guests," he said. She called Massey's office, and we waited for several minutes until he appeared.

"Hey, John... hi, folks, I'm Bruce Massey. Come on back."

The four of us headed down a marbled corridor. "How do you like our new look?" Massey asked as he turned to Hill for a response.

"Major upgrade. Quite different from my last time here. Business must be good," Hill said, smiling as we entered Massey's office.

"It is, I'm happy to say. The best job security a guy like me could have. Coffee, anyone?" Massey asked.

"No, thanks, we just had breakfast," I responded.

"Please, have a seat."

"John, I understand you have some photos you want to share, and please forgive me, ladies, for not saying this earlier. I'm so sorry to hear about what happened to you both."

"Thank you," my mother and I replied.

Hill started. "Bruce, we have something huge here. There's something evil taking place in the city, and we have the evidence to prove it. See, the supposedly vacant house next door to where Alexis lives, and where she was taken to, is a cover-up for some criminal enterprise that involves the police, city officials and probably anyone else around here on the wrong side of the law. We were able to get inside and saw some of the most horrific things you could imagine. Take a look at these pictures." Hill scrolled through the photos on his cell phone before turning on his camcorder to show Massey the footage taken.

"Oh my, this is awful!" Massey blurted as he glanced at the grisly snapshots of the severed heads in the duffel bag, the plastic packages of cocaine, heroin and marijuana, the women and girls held in captivity, and the arsenal of weapons in the containers.

"Shockingly, they had her mother bound and gagged in a utility closet," Hill said as he pointed to my mother. "And unbelievably, they've set up what looks like an underground city, with cars, trucks and who knows what else beneath that house."

Hill took in a deep breath and leaned back in his chair. "So that house is nothing more than a camouflaged entrance to a world of organized crime," he said.

"This is unbelievable, John. I'm going to work with my team to put together a story for our syndicated show, *Straightline* with Maria Copeland, our top anchor. I'll have to get senior approval first. It shouldn't be a problem, since we don't have to deal with some of the same bullshit bureaucracy that many of our competitors do. Please excuse my French, ladies."

"Good, good," Hill said and nodded.

"At the same time, I'll call some of my contacts in Washington to get some interest," Massey said. "Of course, we'll have to be particular about who we talk to. We never know who's on the other side," he added as he smiled coyly at Hill.

"Let us know if you need anything else," said Hill.

"Can I keep these?" Massey asked, as he held up Hill's cell.

"Sure," Hill replied, his face showing signs of relief and less stress now.

"I'll have my assistant download them before you leave."

"Good, let us know how things progress," Hill said as we all shook hands.

CHAPTER 5

THE NEXT THREE weeks saw a media frenzy as investigative reporters began the arduous task of secretly following Crowley and several of his fellow officers. At night, at least two of them would camp out in the 200 block of Mulholland Drive in an inconspicuous white van equipped with telescoping cameras, looking to capture video surveillance footage, and anything that could help expose the alleged corruption.

Crowley and his partners in crime were now more cautious than ever and planned to stay out of sight until some of the dust settled. The reporters, relentless in their search for answers, remained committed. As they sat in the vehicle with their ears to the ground, suddenly, over their scanner came a report of shots fired in the Forest Hills subdivision several miles away. A quiet, upscale community with two-story contemporary homes and neatly manicured lawns, Forest Hills was home to many of the city's policemen and firemen and numerous elected officials, such as Alderman Bill Dunleavy.

"Shots fired! Shots fired!" the police dispatcher blurted repeatedly. "All available units to the scene of 3110 Oakridge Drive. Officer inside, status of injuries or fatalities unknown at this time."

The reporters, sensing there might be some connection to the case, set down their surveillance equipment and raced to the crime scene. As they approached, they were quickly turned back and instructed to keep a certain distance. A Lake Park PD sergeant was given the daunting task of controlling the situation, adding frustration to a face already rife with agitation.

The sergeant barked: "This is an active crime scene, ladies and gentlemen. Inside this perimeter is only for those in law enforcement. Please back up and remain behind that barricade across the street. *It's for your own safety, dammit!*"

The two reporters parked their van and climbed out with their binoculars, managing to look over the crowd of onlookers. The front picture window of 3110 Oakridge Drive had been completely obliterated with some type of high-powered weapons. Yellow crime tape surrounded the house as evidence technicians scoured the premises. One of the reporters padded back to the news van to pick up police and EMS feeds on the scanner. There were different channels and various feeds broadcasting conflicting information, but after several minutes, the right frequency was dialed in quickly.

One of the detectives walked over to a uniformed cop standing in the driveway. "Captain, we've got something here. It looks like these could be from an AR-15,"

"No shit. You had a chance to talk to him yet?"

"No, once we finish processing, we're going to talk to him. See what he knows, and if he's got a clue who might be involved."

Department personnel hurried back and forth as detectives sought out potential witnesses. More news media trucks quickly arrived on location, with each network's reporters jockeying for position.

The live reporting began.

"We're here at the scene of a shooting in the 3100 block of Oak Ridge Drive in the Forest Hills subdivision, involving the home of Lake Park Police Officer Mike Crowley. Witnesses tell us that a dark-colored SUV, possibly black with tinted windows, slowly drove by just as night fell, and that is when several of the vehicle's occupants began firing some type of high-powered weapons at the officer's home, shattering the front picture window. Sources tell us that no one was harmed in the incident, and police are currently searching for the vehicle. We'll keep you updated as new details emerge. Stay tuned for more information at ten."

As the reporter prepared to leave, someone noticed neighborhood resident Alderman Bill Dunleavy standing on the curb across the street. The reporter yelled, "Alderman Dunleavy, you got a minute?"

"Sure, but I'll only talk to you off camera," he said.

Several reporters rushed across the street to begin their questioning.

"Alderman, are you shocked that this shooting occurred in your neighborhood?"

"It's very unusual to say the least. Can't say we're used to this in Forest Hills. However, considering who's involved, I can't say that I'm totally surprised."

"Really?" The reporter smiled as if caught completely off guard. "Care to elaborate?"

"Well, let's just say the chickens may be coming home to roost. And I'll leave it at that."

"Are you saying that whoever did the shooting, in your opinion, had Crowley as the target, sir?"

"Look, I'm not saying that I know that as fact. But what I do know is that, when you mess over enough people, pretty soon someone's gonna come knocking. And that's all I have to say regarding the matter. Good evening, gentlemen," Dunleavy said as he turned to walk toward his house.

The reporters and cameramen strolled back to their van and were quickly approached by two investigative reporters from Harbor Media Group.

"Gentlemen, I'm Harvey Millsap and this is Michael Pomper. We're working on a piece regarding allegations of misconduct involving Mike Crowley."

"Well, well, join the club. If what they're saying about this guy is true, he must be the pride and joy of the department."

"Yeah, we just talked to one of the neighbors, an Alderman Dunleavy, and he had nothing fond to say about Crowley."

"Dunleavy… Dunleavy, hey, that name rings a bell. Wasn't there a story about his wife having an affair with some cop? I think it damned near derailed his campaign. I felt sorry for the guy."

"Well, was it Crowley?"

"Don't know. They never revealed the identity of the cop."

"Yeah, I wonder why. This guy seems well connected."

As the news crews prepared to leave, several officers and one detective remained on the scene to talk to Crowley. It had been a long day, and the recent crime wave in the city had taken a toll on the police. Many seemed agitated and more impatient than usual.

One detective, Ray Silva, a twenty-five-year veteran of the department, trudged in the house after talking to several neighbors, and summoned other officers from outside to join in. They entered the home through the living room, walked to the kitchen, and pulled out wheeled chairs from underneath a contemporary glass table to take a seat.

"Crowley, got any ideas about who could have done this?" one of the cops asked.

"I suspect it could be one of many punks we've taken off the street recently. They could've Googled my name and found out where I live. As you guys know, we've put a dent in their operation. Drugs, guns, gangs, it's the same shit everywhere. I do know one thing, though, I'm going to work my contacts on the street and find out exactly what we're dealing with here. Targeting me is one thing, but now they're bold enough to come to my house? All options are on the table as far as I'm concerned," he said belligerently.

One of the investigative officers quickly responded: "You're best to let us handle this the right way or things could get really ugly, Crowley. We're keeping a marked car on the street, around the clock protection if necessary. Keep in touch and let us know if you come up with any leads. And if your wife and kids have someplace else they can go until this thing simmers down, that wouldn't be a bad idea either."

"Okay, will do."

The officers left, and crime scene techs began wrapping up their analysis of the premises. As soon as the coast cleared, Crowley ran downstairs into his basement, angrily knocking over chairs and anything else in his way. Suddenly, he felt an excruciating pain in his arm, the type he had been experiencing more and more frequently, ever since he had been involved in an off-duty car accident with a reckless driver. A thorough medical examination would soon be necessary, he thought.

Earlier, he'd purposely failed to mention his high-tech camera and surveillance system to the responding officers. The system was installed to be hidden from view and, if working as intended, could help him determine who had done the shooting.

Crowley powered on a seventeen-inch widescreen monitor and restarted the recorded segment to play. The captured video was dark and somewhat grainy. No sound could be heard. As the tape rolled, a slow-moving vehicle could be seen entering the frame. It was a dark-colored SUV, possibly a late model Range Rover. As the vehicle crept by, the rear window was lowered and the barrels of several automatic weapons could be seen pointing towards the house. The flash of gunfire lit up the frame, as round after round was fired directly into the front picture window.

He watched the footage, hoping to get a glance of the vehicle's occupants, but the lighting was too dark and the video too grainy. As the vehicle roared off after the shooting, Crowley paused the recording to get a glimpse of the license plate, which could barely be seen. L5192K48, it looked like to his trained eye. With a plate number to go on, he contacted one of his accomplices who worked inside the department for help. He was pissed and determined to get to these assholes before his colleagues did.

Phil Slauson had worked for the department for twenty-eight years and was close to retirement, with a wife and two kids in college. He couldn't afford to let some bullshit or other misconduct end his career prematurely. But this was Mike Crowley who needed help, off the record. Crowley had been instrumental in helping Slauson get considered for promotions in the past. So when Crowley called, Slauson performed the search.

"Bingo, you lucky shit! I've got a hit on that plate. It belongs to a Rico Alcazar, home address of 11203 Washington Boulevard, Apartment B. It's over in the Wicker Park area. You know where that's at?"

"Yeah, I know where that is."

"A word of caution, though. This guy's got some rap sheet, Mike, including a prior for attempted murder. Be careful."

"Phil, thanks much. You're the man. I'll talk to you later."

"Will do, my friend," said Slauson.

"The nerve of that fucker," Crowley shouted after ending the call. Well aware of who Alcazar was, Crowley was fuming. Alcazar was one of his main connections to the city's underworld, a large network of buyers for the goods and services of Crowley's criminal enterprise. He pulled out his phone and made the call.

"Wassup," snapped Alcazar.

"You shoot up my house, you fucking moron? What's your problem?!"

"Whoa! Whoa! And good morning to you too, you piece of shit! Look, Crowley, I represent a lot of unhappy people. You've got their money, and they're pissed. Consider what happened a warning. Hey, I had no choice. I just do what I'm told. Go with the flow and everybody's happy. Deliver the goods and we're good."

"Look, I told you assholes it would take some time. We're waiting on more product to come in. Now because of you fuckers and that nurse bitch, I've got the spotlight on my ass. Tell your people to calm down. I'll get their stuff within a week. Most of this shit comes from other places, so it takes longer, but they'll get it!"

"Alright, Crowley, the ball's in your court. You know how to reach me." They both ended the call on their encrypted disposable cell phones. Crowley then made several other calls, one to put a rush on the incoming product, the other to put an end to a problem.

The investigation was gaining momentum at Harbor Media Group. Investigative journalists assigned to the story were uncovering crucial details, including researching city records for the now-infamous house on Mulholland Drive. Bruce Massey, satisfied with his team's progress, called for an impromptu meeting to discuss details about the investigation. Entering the conference room were various field reporters, including the two at the scene of the shooting, a new intern assigned to clerical and administrative duties, and Maria Copeland, the accomplished on-air personality who would feature the story on national TV. Massey entered the room with a cup of Starbucks, making adjustments on his laptop for a PowerPoint presentation.

"Hello, everyone. I wanted to go over some highlights and address any concerns that you may have. Our investigation is moving forward quite well. However, we must all keep in mind that we are dealing with our local police department instead of civilians. That being said, I put together this presentation, which will help us to focus on the key points of the story.

"Point number one: Officer Mike Crowley is our primary focus, despite others being possibly involved. We need as many facts as possible to support our theory about his involvement in these crimes and this criminal enterprise.

"Point number two: we need to keep as much of our investigation as confidential as possible. We don't know who we're talking to that might be the eyes and ears of Crowley and his cohorts.

"Point number three: we need to protect the identities of our witnesses for their own safety.

"Point number four: any inquiries from the feds need to go through my office first.

"And point number five: each one of you watch your back out there. We're dealing with some seriously ruthless people who'll stop at nothing to put a lid on our efforts. That's it for now."

Mike Crowley could have cared less that the focus on him was intensifying. He wanted to find Rico Alcazar and return the favor. A call was made to set up a meeting at the house on Mulholland.

"Yeah, I got those things you wanted. I need you to meet me at the spot," said Crowley to Alcazar from his disposable cell.

"What time?"

"Twenty-one hundred. Call and I'll let you in."

"Okay, cool."

Nine p.m. arrived as Alcazar and two of his partners in crime drove up to the house in a silver Chevy Silverado and parked near the corner. The house was mostly dark except for a glimpse of light illuminating in the rear. Alcazar shut off the engine and made the call.

"Yo, Crowley, I'm outside. You here?"

"Yeah, come to the back, the gate's open."

Alcazar and his crew climbed out of their vehicle and walked to the back of the house, stepping over garbage while trying to make out the silhouette of whoever was holding the door open. One by one, the men stepped inside and were greeted by Crowley.

"Follow me. The stuff's downstairs in one of the rooms."

The men walked toward the basement. "This place stinks," one of Alcazar's partners whispered to the other while holding a hand to his nose.

"Okay, this is what I've got so far," said Crowley as he opened one of the wooden containers in the room. He then reached in and quickly pulled out a semiautomatic pistol, complete with suppressor, and with several quick taps to the chest, Alcazar and the other two men dropped to the floor.

Crowley knew the execution was hurting his operation in the long run. Alcazar was a liaison to a lot of clients in Chicago, but it was more important to him that a message be sent that Crowley and his family were not to be harmed or threatened.

He summoned several of his cohorts to help with the disposal of the bodies, which were wrapped in plastic bags and taken to the Underground, a code word for the lower level beneath the basement.

Later that night, he received an ominous phone call from a mystery caller. The call went straight to voicemail with the following message:

"Crowley, we've been watching developments and things have gotten way out of hand. You've created a mess and now you need to fix it. We trusted you. You were our eyes and ears on the street. Those witnesses need to be dealt with before there's any trial. Either you take care of them now, and clean things up fast... or consider your days numbered." Click.

Crowley knew with dead certainty that his first priority would be to find Alexis Fields, the potentially, key witness. His looming incarceration or acquittal rested in her hands. The following morning he called Slauson for unofficial information. Slauson was being kept up-to-date about the investigation and could easily obtain information regarding the case, including where it was headed next.

"Phil, it's Mike. Listen, I need another favor. I need you to find out the whereabouts of Alexis Fields. She's a key witness in my case. I know it's putting you on a limb. Once I'm through this, I owe you big time, my friend."

"Alright, Mike, but this has got to be the last time. Because of this case, we've all got eyes on us. I love you, brother, but I ain't going down for nobody!"

"I know, I know, and that's exactly why finding her is so important."

"Okay, I should have something by tomorrow afternoon at the latest. I'll check with my guys, including SOS, and I'll call you."

"Thanks," Crowley said.

He could afford to wait for Slauson's call. He had taken time off after his house was targeted in the drive-by. And it was time to tie up loose ends and make good on his promise to the people he was indebted to. A call came in from some other cops asking if he wanted to hang out at one of their favorite watering holes. Crowley wasn't a heavy drinker. He would keep company on occasion at a local sports bar called DJ's, which was also a popular stomping ground among Lake Park's finest. However, he wasn't in the mood for this outing and didn't need the unwanted attention. He quickly responded that this "wasn't a good night, maybe next time." After watching details of the case on the local news, he spent time with his family and went to bed.

CHAPTER **6**

THE FOLLOWING MORNING, the call came in from Slauson.

"Mike, she's staying at the Radisson Plaza Hotel over on Delaney Avenue near downtown. Room 318. She's been advised to go under an assumed name. Her mother is supposedly in town and staying with her as well. Wait, there's more," Slauson said, as he tried to decipher his own scribbled handwriting. "It looks like she's being helped by some guy named John Hill, who went to a Harbor Media Group to run a story about the case. Intel also says that the main guy in charge over at Harbor Media goes by the name of Bruce Massey. This Massey guy has some political aspirations and wants to blow the case wide open with some help from the feds."

"You got Hill and Massey's addresses?" Crowley asked.

"Sure do, Hill resides at 51 Covington Rd in Cooperstown and Massey resides at 3630 Wakaugna Circle in the Deerfield Estates subdivision."

"Got it. Thanks again, bro."

Now that Crowley knew their whereabouts, everyone was considered fair game. The investigation was gaining full steam, and Harbor Media was completing the segment to be aired on national TV. It was only a matter of time before indictments were handed down. And Crowley was well aware—he had been in the game too long not to know how things worked.

Then it struck him—a planned hit list targeted by some gang members who owed him a favor. He quickly called Slauson back.

"John, you still got the info up on that guy Massey?"

"Yeah, I got it right here."

"Any priors?"

"Let's see… four years ago he was arrested for a DUI and resisting arrest. Oh, and here, last summer, arrested for public intoxication in Indiana. Charges were later dropped."

"Okay, and what about Hill?"

"Nothing, nada."

"And Fields?"

"Clean as a whistle. Mike, as your friend, heed my warning. You've got eyes on you. You're better off letting someone else handle these matters. This place may be crawling with feds soon."

"I'm already on it. And I know just who to call for the job. Talk to you later."

Most of the city's gang members and drug dealers knew about Crowley's organization. He supplied weapons when they needed them, and would tip them off to any potential police activity. He figured it was payback time, and in order to talk to his contact, he would have to drive to the city's perilous west side and ask for him. The gang, known as the B.P. Hustlers, didn't use phones to communicate, and knew, with good reason, that their calls would've been electronically monitored.

Crowley pulled up to the Brookstone Public Housing projects, whose two-story brick buildings, featured graffiti-covered walls and hallways that reeked of urine. Residents were closely watching him, knowing he wasn't from around here.

A teenager sporting dreadlocks, jeans and a faded sweatshirt quickly stopped while on his Schwinn.

"Hey, you know where I can find Derek Sparks?" Crowley asked the teen, still sitting on his bike.

"Who's looking for him?" the boy asked.

"Tell him Crowley—he and his crew know me as Bogeyman."

The boy looked bewildered.

"But don't tell anybody else. That's a secret between you and me," Crowley said as he smiled at the kid.

"Alright, wait here. I'll be back."

The teenager, apparently sensing some urgency in Crowley's visit, hurried off his bike and ran halfway up the stairs inside.

"Yo, D... there's somebody out here to see you. Says his name is the Bogeyman," the boy shouted up into the hallway. Several minutes later, running down the steps was Derek Sparks, aka. D-Man. He was shirtless, his hair braided in cornrows, and tattoos covered most of his slim, muscular frame. Sparks was a two-time convicted felon whom Crowley had encountered during a neighborhood drug sweep.

"What up, C? Long time no see. What brings you to this side of town?" Sparks said as the two embraced.

Crowley grinned widely, squinting into the glare of the sun. "I need a favor. I got some people trying to take me down. I need you and your crew to handle it for me. I can't have any loose ends. They're witnesses in my case, trying to bring in the feds." Crowley scanned the area as he pulled out a handwritten list on a sheet of paper. "These are the names and addresses," he said.

Sparks lowered his gaze as he studied the list.

Crowley patted Sparks's chest with the back of his hand. "I figure you guys owe me, so after this we can call it even," he said as his voice got louder. "You go back to doing what you do. I go back to my family, and everyone has a nice life! You know what I mean?"

"Yeah, I know. I feel you. Don't worry, we got you on this. I'll let you know when it's done."

"Okay, let me know," Crowley said.

"Alright, for sure."

As Crowley padded back to his car to head home, he knew better than to tell anyone. Not even his partners in crime would be privy to his fiendishly arranged hit list. The fewer people who knew, the better off things would be.

CHAPTER 7

IT WAS SEVERAL weeks since Hill, my mother, and I had met with Bruce Massey at Harbor Media Group. I waited patiently for the investigation to develop. Still off from work, I contemplated my future and worried about the safety of my mother, who remained in town.

As I finished completing some documents for work a text came in from Hill...

The story will be on this week's episode of Straightline, Friday at 8 p.m. on Channel 5.

This was touted as a highly anticipated episode, as news of the story and subsequent investigation spread all over the media. There was no turning back. Several days went by. I had urged my mother to return home, where she would be safer, but she was firm on her decision to stay. The two of us stayed holed up in our hotel room for most of the day, only venturing out when necessary.

Then came the breaking news report on the room's television.

"A local media executive was found beaten to death in front of his home in Deerfield Estates. Police say fifty-two-year-old Bruce Massey was found by his neighbor, lying in a pool of blood in his driveway after apparently suffering blunt force trauma to the head. Police are releasing few details at the moment, and no one is in custody at this time. Stay tuned for more details at nine."

My mother and I stared at the newscast in disbelief, momentarily unable to speak. Suddenly, my emotions took a turn for the worse.

"*Oh, my God!* I can't believe it. They killed him! *I know they killed him!* I'm calling John… I've got to contact him, in case he doesn't know."

Visibly shaken, I looked for my cell to call Hill. Unable to reach him, I left an unnerving message on his voicemail: "John, this is Alexis. We just heard on the news that *Bruce Massey was murdered!* Please call right away. And be safe."

My mother and I wondered in terrifying silence who was next. Five minutes later, the call came in from Hill.

"John, thank God you're okay. Are you watching the news? This is unbelievable."

"I got your voicemail and I'm at a loss for words. I… I can't believe this either. I *just* talked to him yesterday, when he told me the story would be airing soon. This is awful. I'll call his office to see what more I can find out. I'm sure those scumbags had something to do with this. It's best that we stay out of sight for a while. You guys should consider moving to a different hotel. They probably know where you're staying by now. Tell the front desk not to give out any information, and that you want all calls and visitors screened."

"And what are *you* doing to stay safe?"

"I have a brother who lives roughly twenty miles away in Waukegan with his wife and kids. I might stay with them for a while. Considering the circumstances, I'm sure it will be okay. In the meantime, I'm going to find out more about what happened to Bruce and what the police know."

"Okay, be safe."

CHAPTER **8**

THE EMPLOYEES AT Harbor Media were in chaos. One of their top executives had been murdered, just as one of the firm's most anticipated stories was about to air. Executives and employees were scrambling, trying to balance inquiries from law enforcement and last-minute preparations before the segment went live.

A call came in from John Hill to Bruce Massey's assistant. Still shaken from the death of her boss, she agreed to talk to Hill briefly about what she knew. After composing herself momentarily, she brought Hill on the line.

"Hi, Mr. Hill, this is Kim Phillips."

"Kim, I'm so terribly sorry to hear about Bruce. It's unbelievable."

"It truly is. We're still in total shock; it's so unreal. I know it sounds clichéd, but he really was a good person and didn't deserve this."

"I agree wholeheartedly. Had anyone called or came to visit him that seemed suspicious, or had he said anything about being afraid recently?"

"None that I'm aware of. Understandably, they're being tight-lipped and certainly not telling us everything, especially with us being part of the media."

"I'm going to find out all I can and help in any way possible. I'll keep in touch. Please inform me of the arrangements."

"I sure will, Mr. Hill. Thank you for calling."

Hill, Alexis, and her mother all made plans to relocate, even if temporarily. It was only a matter of time before their lives were placed in imminent danger. Due to the nature of the case, the police were informed that the FBI would also be part of the investigation. They would leave no stone unturned regarding the circumstances surrounding Massey's murder.

Many questions remained unanswered:

Was he involved in any personal relationships?

Had he received any death threats?

Did he have any known enemies or confrontations?

Was he involved in any illicit behavior that no one knew about?

All the police knew were the brutal details of the attack, that Massey had been hit repeatedly with some sort of blunt object, fracturing his skull and orbital socket and causing massive trauma. Nothing of value had been taken, and the police had concluded that robbery was not a motive. But investigators were relentless in their quest to apprehend whoever was responsible. Even Massey's coworkers were considered fair game.

Massey had lived alone at the time of his murder and had no relatives living in close proximity. Homicide detectives scoured his home and office looking for clues, to no avail. Computers and other items were taken in for analysis as potentially key in the investigation.

Eventually, John Hill was contacted and asked for an interview. Hill obliged and agreed to meet with investigators; however, only on the condition that someone from the FBI be present. Although the meeting would take place at a different police district than the one Crowley worked in, Hill wasn't taking any chances. He knew it was likely someone from Crowley's district would be there as well. The meeting was scheduled for 9:30 the following morning at the police station on Wakaugna Boulevard.

"Good morning, Mr. Hill. Thanks for your cooperation. Have a seat. Coffee?"

"No, thanks… just had breakfast."

"My name is Todd Capelli, this is Detective Ray Silva, and that's FBI Agent Preston Ponder, here at your request. I want to inform you that we'll be recording this interview and everything you say will be made part of the record. Are you ready?"

"Sure," Hill said.

Ponder pressed record and spun around the small Sony digital recorder that was lying on the conference table, then stated: "The following is a brief interview with Mr. John Hill regarding the death of Bruce Massey, Hines County Case Number M843W59. Mr. Hill, what was the nature of your relationship with Mr. Massey?"

"We were friends, attended college together in Boston, and kept in touch ever since."

"Do you know why anyone would want to harm him?"

"Well, he was working on airing a story about Officer Mike Crowley and his alleged involvement with the sexual assault of Alexis Fields, as well as a number of other criminal offenses. He also planned to seek help at the federal level with the case."

"And why is that?"

"He figured, if the local police department were in charge of investigating themselves, then the case wouldn't go very far."

"Did he ever mention to you that he might be in some kind of trouble, or danger?"

"No, not really. I think his main concern was Crowley, and the police looking out for one of their own."

"I understand that you know Ms. Fields personally."

"Yes, that's true."

"Are you romantically involved with her?"

"No, we're friends. It's strictly platonic."

"Mr. Hill, where were you the night that Mr. Massey was murdered?"

Hill leaned forward, glaring intently. "Wait a minute—am I being considered a suspect now?"

"Not at all. Simply routine questions we need to ask."

"With all due respect, gentlemen, I really don't care to proceed with this interview without having an attorney present."

Capelli glanced with distaste at Silva and Ponder.

"Alright, we appreciate your stopping by today. We'll be in touch, if necessary," Capelli said.

Hill stood and said, "I'm here to help solve the case any way I can. He was a dear friend."

"I understand. We'll do our best."

Hill shook hands with each of the men before leaving the conference room to head to the parking lot, when he received the text regarding Massey's funeral.

Arrangements for Bruce will be Friday, 11 a.m. at Brower Bros. funeral home.

He forwarded the text to Alexis, who had been preparing to move to a different hotel with her mother.

I'll pick you guys up. We can all go together, Hill added.

We'll see you then. Perhaps nine or ten?

Will do, Hill texted back.

The pace of the investigation continued to intensify as the local community, including law enforcement, anxiously awaited Friday's airing of *Straightline*. The employees at Harbor Media Group were frantically working to meet last-minute deadlines while still reeling from the untimely death of their boss.

Friday would be a day of mixed emotions, Hill thought. It would be the day that would finally expose the city's rampant corruption, but would also be the day that his friend would be laid to rest.

Hill arrived at the Country Inn Suites parking lot in his SUV just before 10 a.m. After driving around for several minutes, he found a parking space near the front entrance to the hotel's lobby.

Quickly pulling out his cell, he sent a text to Alexis, telling her he was downstairs waiting. Five minutes later, Alexis and her mother exited the hotel elevator and headed toward a set of sliding glass doors.

CHAPTER 9

WE WALKED OUT of the hotel lobby and into the parking lot as Hill wheeled around.

"There he is," I said.

My mother and I were dressed in business casual attire and heels. We headed toward his vehicle.

"Good morning."

"Morning, ladies. How are you holding up so far?"

"We're okay, considering the circumstances."

"Looking forward to putting this entire ordeal behind us."

Hill rechecked the GPS on his phone for directions to the funeral home before we pulled out of the parking lot. As we weaved through the congested streets, we talked of how the situation's outcome could, in fact, lead us down uncertain paths.

"I had a meeting with the police and answered some of their questions about Bruce," he said.

"Any leads or motives yet?" I asked.

"Not yet—at least, not that they told me. But that's how the police are. They don't divulge everything they know."

"I wonder if they suspect Crowley had something to do with Bruce's murder?" I said.

"Not sure if they do, but I don't trust them, and I requested that someone from the FBI sit in on the interview. And you know what, they obliged, most likely since the FBI is now part of the investigation, too. They wanted to record everything as well. But I also requested they stop the interview once they asked about my whereabouts the night Bruce was killed."

"You should have had an attorney present, John. I'm consulting with one now, actually," I told him.

"I know. I should have. I figured *I* wasn't a suspect, and perhaps didn't need counsel. Besides, they aren't cheap, even if for one day."

It was 10:40 a.m. now, and traffic on the highway was at a standstill due to an accident ahead and corresponding gapers delay.

"I think I should exit here and take the streets, or we won't make it in time," said Hill.

We maneuvered through the clog and exited onto Independence Boulevard. We arrived at the funeral home within fifteen minutes, parked, and went inside, where we were greeted and instructed where to sit. An instrumental version of a moving religious song trumpeted over the funeral parlor's speakers as mourners viewed the body in a single-file line.

There were friends, family, coworkers, colleagues, media and even some of Massey's competitors there to pay their respects. After a minister's thoughtful words of comfort came performances from a local choir. At the family's request, I'd been told. There were poems and acknowledgments, and not a dry eye inside, as those who knew Massey said their final good-byes.

Due to the nature of his death and because it was so unexpected, the service was emotionally gut-wrenching.

Hill had asked if he could say a few words and was motioned to come forward when it was his turn to speak. I watched as he stood behind the podium, tissue in hand as he tried his best to choke back tears.

"They say in life that if you have *one* true friend, you're blessed. I feel confident in saying today that Bruce was that friend. Was he perfect? No, none of us are. Did he make mistakes? Sure, we all do. But if you knew Bruce the way I did, and was touched by his kind spirit and warm personality, you too would be happy to call him a true friend. I will miss him dearly."

Everyone in attendance clapped as Hill left the podium to return to his seat. As the service concluded, mourners greeted each other and prepared to leave for the cemetery to attend the burial.

We left the building to walk toward Hill's SUV in the parking lot when we noticed a suspicious-looking car, a maroon Chevy Impala with matching rims and slightly tinted windows, slowly driving by. Whoever was inside was observing the mourners as we exited the building.

Undaunted, we climbed into Hill's Ford Explorer and talked, as Hill checked his phone's GPS for directions to the cemetery.

"We can get there in, like, forty minutes depending on traffic," he said.

"You think it's safe? We're gonna be outside," I said.

"Well, you would *think* it's safe at a cemetery. But things happen at the most unlikely places these days. That car that went by looked really suspicious. Although it looks like whoever it was is gone now."

One of the staffers from the funeral home, an older gentleman with white hair in a black suit, walked over to Hill's vehicle as we waited in the lot. "Sir, you have a sticker for your windshield?" he asked.

"No, we need one."

"Here, just peel off the tape and put it in the lower corner on the passenger side. We're going to line up in front and leave from there." The man handed the orange decal to Hill.

"Okay, thanks."

Once we were in line, the hearse and all the vehicles that followed proceeded to Oakmount Cemetery. The burial lasted twenty minutes, and then everyone went back to their vehicles to go home.

"Since tonight is the airing of *Straightline*, I set my DVR to record it," Hill said as he opened the doors for my mother and me. We then drove for several blocks, looking for a nearby restaurant to grab a quick lunch. At the request of Massey's family, there had been no repast.

"What did you guys have a taste for?" Hill asked.

"It doesn't matter, as long as it's good," I replied.

"I know this nice and cozy comfort food place, not too expensive," he said as we gradually approached the intersection on North Fremont Avenue, stopping for a light.

"So what do you ladies think?" he asked while looking in his rearview, then the side-view mirror, peering at the ominous vehicle slowly approaching on the left. I couldn't believe it—it was the same maroon Chevy Impala. There was no doubt in my mind that these were the same suspicious characters that we'd seen earlier. My heart beat faster.

In what seemed like a split second later, the window of the Chevy Impala rolled down, and out came a large black handgun, blasting four shots into the driver's-side door of Hill's Explorer. The Impala then sped off, tires screeching while running through the red light. My mother and I were screaming and hysterical. We both bolted from the vehicle, running into a nearby convenience store for help.

"Please help us, our friend has been shot! Someone please call the police!"

The store clerk yelled, "C'mon, wait back here. I'll call for you!" while motioning us in his direction, probably wanting to protect us from further harm. We followed him and scurried to the back of the store, into a room that looked like some sort of storage space turned makeshift office. The clerk nervously pulled out his cell phone and dialed.

"911, what's your emergency?"

"Yes, I have some people here in my store who said that their friend was just shot outside."

"Are they in the store now?"

"Yes."

"What's your exact location, sir?"

"2516 North Fremont Ave—Dave's Stop & Go."

"Has anyone else been shot?"

"No, not that I'm aware of."

"Where is the victim?"

"I believe right outside the store."

"Okay, police are on their way. Please stay inside and lock the doors if possible."

Several minutes later, an ambulance and police cruisers had converged onto Fremont Ave. Paramedics quickly got Hill out of the vehicle. My mother and I followed the EMTs, asking if Hill was okay while trying to describe to the detectives what had happened. The police were asking questions. CSI types were all over the place. It was complete chaos.

"Is he going to be okay? Is he going to make it?" we called out as we watched Hill being strapped to a gurney.

"He's been hit once, it looks like. They're rushing him to the hospital now. We're told the other bullets missed him," one of the officers said.

"Oh, thank God. We need to get to the hospital. Where are they taking him?" I asked one of the cops.

"Just hold tight. We'll let you know in a few minutes," he snapped.

The officer talked to several other cops before coming back to speak to my mother and me.

A tall, imposing man suddenly approached. "Ma'am, I'm Officer Jim Belden," he said with a voice that cracked the air like thunder. "I need to know exactly what happened here. Just start from the beginning."

"We were stopped at the light, talking in the vehicle, and this other car pulled up to the side of us and started shooting for no reason," I said.

"The make, model…color?"

"It was a Chevy Impala. The color was maroon."

"Plate?"

"No, sir."

"Any description of the attackers?"

"No, everything happened so fast, we just cowered when they started shooting."

"Your friend was taken to Hines County Hospital. Here's the address." Belden handed the scribbled address to me on a small sheet of paper. "Either of you need to go to the hospital for treatment?"

"No, I think we're okay."

"You ladies have someone to pick you up? Need a ride to the hospital to see your friend?"

"We could use a ride. We'd like to check up on him," I said.

"I have to go that way. I'll be happy to drop you both off. Just give me a minute to wrap things up here," the big cop said.

We both stood by his cruiser as he went inside the store to talk to the clerk. Moments later, he came outside.

"All set, ready to go," he said.

My mother and I climbed inside Belden's cruiser, curiously gazing at the various gadgets, lights and equipment built into the vehicle's dashboard.

"Are you ladies from around the area?"

"I recently relocated here, and my mom's visiting from Wisconsin."

"My guess is you don't have a favorable impression of Lake Park at this point."

"It's been a challenge, to say the least."

"Any idea why someone would want to hurt your friend?"

"Well, probably because we're part of an effort involving exposing alleged corruption in the city, and our friend is a key part of the investigation."

My mother glanced at me as if to indicate to be careful and not talk too much. She was probably right—this *was* still a cop we were talking to, even though he obviously worked out of a different district than Crowley.

"It's clear he was targeted. Hopefully we'll catch whoever was responsible, and the animals will be brought to justice," Belden said.

"We hope so. Ironically, we'd just come from the funeral of *another* person we knew, who was murdered."

"Wow, you think the two crimes are related? Same people responsible?" Belden asked.

"That seems very plausible," I said.

Processing all the information that we'd been giving, Belden seemed to become more intrigued by what he was hearing. "This city has never seen so many murders occur as it has in the preceding twelve months," he said.

Peering out of the side window, I could see the brightly displayed name and signage of the hospital as we got closer.

"I'll go in with you ladies to check up on him," Belden said. We all hurried through the sliding glass doors of the emergency room and asked one of the nurses about Hill.

"He's in surgery right now. It's going to be a while. You can wait over there if you'd like," the nurse said and pointed to some blue conjoined seats in the waiting area.

"Do you know his condition?" I asked, my eyes starting to well with tears, while hoping for a favorable response.

"From what I'm told, and don't quote me on this, the bullet went through the front of his abdomen, but didn't hit any vital organs. He's extremely fortunate. To me, it sounds more like a flesh wound. I think he's going to be alright. I'll keep you updated with his progress."

"Thank you."

My mother, Belden and I waited patiently for more than an hour and a half for the doctor or one of the nurses to come forth with additional details. Finally, there was an update. Dr. Francis Neuremberg, a tall, lanky man with salt-and-pepper hair and a quirky walk, sauntered down the hall to the waiting area to introduce himself.

"Hi, folks. Are you all here for John Hill?" he asked.

"Yes, how is he?"

"He'll be fine. He's lost some blood and has been going in and out of consciousness. However, he's stabilized and we anticipate that he'll make a full recovery. He's truly blessed that things were not a lot worse. Lately, we've seen a higher than usual number of gunshot victims. A sign of the times, it seems. You'll be able to see him hopefully today, once the nurses and I are finished treating him."

"Thanks so much, Doctor, we appreciate your efforts," I said.

Belden looked down at his watch, probably realizing that his time spent at the hospital would have to be cut short. He stood up, towering over us as we stayed seated.

"Ladies, I'm going to have to leave. I was hoping to be able to stick around to see Mr. Hill, but I have to get back. Our department has been short on manpower lately. We've had some guys retire, and they haven't hired any replacements. They claim the money's just not there, which, if you ask me, is total BS."

"Well, we appreciate your concern, and thank you for bringing us to the hospital."

"Are you both gonna be okay getting home? If not, there's a decent hotel around the corner," Belden said.

"We'll see how it goes with our friend; we may actually be *here* all night."

"I wish Mr. Hill the best. Godspeed. It was nice meeting you both."

"Thanks again," I replied.

Belden walked past the nurses' station on the left, passing various rooms and medical equipment in the hallway. My mother and I talked, periodically glancing at the television in the waiting room, while patiently waiting to hear the latest about Hill's condition.

About forty-five minutes later, a nurse's assistant came briskly walking down the hall to the visitors' area.

"Are you ladies here to see John Hill?"

"Yes, ma'am."

"You can come up now. He's been awake, talking and asking for his friends and his brother. The doctor wants to limit his visitation time to give him more time for recovery. So please keep your visit with him somewhat short if possible. He's in room 203. Go down this hall, make a right and take the elevators just past the restrooms. My name is Melissa. I'll be here all night. Just page me if either you or Mr. Hill should need me."

"Thank you, Melissa."

We walked down the hall, mixing in with the rush of medical personnel going back and forth. Hines County Hospital, like others in Lake Park, apparently had been stretched to the limit with everything that had been taking place. The crime, accidents, and incidents of sickness in the city had obviously taken a toll.

We quietly entered room 203 and saw Hill lying in an elevated position, connected to an IV. He appeared either unconscious or asleep. A constant beep could be heard from one of the digital monitors in the room.

"John?" I called quietly.

His eyes slowly opened while gazing forward. He smiled, happy to catch a glimpse of some familiar faces.

"Hey," he said groggily, his voice barely audible as he winced in pain from his injury.

"Glad to see you're going to be okay. We're going to stay here with you, through the night if we have to." We stood by his bed with words of comfort and encouragement. Hill was there for us. Now it was our turn to reciprocate.

CHAPTER 10

THERE WAS A public outcry after the airing of *Straightline*. Local officials, including some politicians, demanded everyone involved in the cover-up be held responsible for their actions. The State's Attorney's Office was salivating; this would be a victory of epic proportions, and the upcoming November elections made the prize even sweeter.

The coming indictments would read like a who's who of the city's elite. The FBI had Crowley and company under surveillance, and had placed informants in the department to identify who the perpetrators were.

There was a meeting between the State's Attorney's Office and the FBI, taking place at the FBI's regional office downtown. Only a select number of members of the media were allowed, and each was advised not to report any details that could jeopardize the integrity of the investigation.

The meeting quickly got underway, with everyone filing into a conference room which held state-of-the-art presentation equipment. A clean-cut fed wearing a dark tailored suit walked to the front of the room.

"Welcome, everyone. Please let me introduce myself. I'm Special Agent in Charge Aaron Torres. To my right is Agent Preston Ponder, and to my left is State's Attorney Nikki Myers and her assistant Liz Shultz. Let me begin by stating that we left no stone unturned in our investigation, and we've uncovered a wealth of information that will be used as evidence in this case.

The crimes that have been committed here are nothing short of appalling, and it disgusts me to no end that these offenders would have the audacity to consider themselves part of law enforcement."

Torres started at the end of the table with laser pointer in hand and walked toward the large white presentation board on the wall. Everyone in the room listened intently as he went into detail, pacing back and forth, sounding much like an attorney during an opening statement. Liz Shultz, the assistant, scribbled notes and jotted down potential questions that would come up later.

"This case started with Mike Crowley, a man who somehow traded in his obligation to serve and protect the citizens of this great city, to become a deviant, a sexual predator, a pimp, a fraud and, as you will find out tonight, a murderer. Any of you remember the case of the Waldrop family that disappeared about a year ago? In case you don't, let me refresh your memory.

"The Waldrops lived at 152 Mulholland Drive for eight years before they disappeared without a trace, never to be seen or heard from again. Just before they disappeared, they made several calls to police about suspicious activity at 158 Mulholland, which is the house next door. The Waldrops were a nice, typical, middle-class family with a seventeen-year-old daughter and no obvious indications of problems in their marriage, according to their relatives, friends and neighbors. At the time of their disappearance, in their home, there were no signs of a struggle and no evidence of foul play, and as of yet, no bodies have turned up anywhere.

"At this time, their whereabouts remain unknown and the case is still open. Now, as for the house next door at 158 Mulholland, we believe that the offenders that are committing criminal activity there are the same ones that are responsible for the disappearance of the Waldrop family. That house was a house of horrors, and serves as the entrance to a criminal enterprise unlike any this city, or perhaps any other city, has ever seen. There were murders taking place, drug trafficking, sex trafficking, including some underage girls, a room where all sorts of illegal weapons were stored for sale, and that's just the beginning.

"There are stairs in the basement that lead to, and get this, an underground city, with paved streets, lights, vehicles and armed men facilitating the criminal activity between Crowley and company and the outside underworld, including many names you would be shocked to see on the list we have. There are politicians, judges, city officials, doctors, lawyers, athletes and some celebrities who are either knowingly or unknowingly willing participants in the grand scheme of things.

"We estimate that this criminal enterprise is taking in at least one million dollars per month. Our investigation reveals that this thing is bigger than any of us had imagined. And that is how they've been able to operate with impunity, until now!" Torres slammed his fist on the presentation board as everyone listened intently.

"With joint cooperation from the State's Attorney's Office, we are preparing to file charges soon in this case. We have evidence that links Crowley to most of it, including the murder of Bruce Massey and the attempted murder of John Hill. We're diligently working on solving the case of the Waldrop family and securing a search warrant for the house at 158 Mulholland. I'll now open it up for any questions."

"Hi, Mr. Torres, my name is Anthony Littlejohn with Harbor Media Group and my question is, with all the murder-suicides occurring among families today, is there enough evidence in the Waldrop case to point to foul play involving someone *outside* of the family, such as Mike Crowley, in contrast to suspecting a spouse or family member?"

"That's a good question, Anthony. What we believe is this: at some point, the Waldrops saw something that put them at risk, and it wasn't until they called police that they disappeared. As you may recall, the exact same thing happened to Ms. Alexis Fields. She lived in the same house, reported suspicious activity next door and was attacked by Crowley and his goons. Fortunately, for her, she survived and was able to escape. Look, this is by no means an easy case. However, I'm confident that the evidence we have is going to be sufficient, in addition to our credible witnesses, and informants we have in place, ready to testify. I'd also like to thank the investigative team of reporters who really did a thorough job in bringing a lot of this information to light. Any more questions?"

"Mr. Torres, Luke Smalls with WYWBN News Network. Do you know at this time exactly how many officers other than Crowley are being implicated in the investigation?"

"Due to the nature of the case, I cannot divulge the exact number, and of course, I can't give out additional names. What I *can* say is that there are a significant number of officers we're looking at bringing charges against, with Crowley being the mastermind behind it all. If there are no further questions, we'll end this meeting for tonight and will keep everyone updated as the investigation progresses."

CHAPTER 11

AFTER THE MEETING with the State's Attorney's Office and the media, Special Agent in Charge Aaron Torres met with his colleagues after completing a conference call with several lead investigators.

"Gentlemen, we have a new development in the Waldrop case. Our agents did some further digging. As it turns out, the neighbor's son across the street, a boy by the name of Brian McKenzie, saw some men escorting the family out of their house. He knew the family well because the Waldrops' daughter used to babysit him when his parents went out on occasion. His exact words were: 'they looked scared,' and he said that Kelly Waldrop, the daughter, 'was crying and trying to pull away from the *bad people*.' He said he watched as they all climbed into a black vehicle, most likely an SUV, and described the vehicle as being large and high up in the air. When investigators initially interviewed neighbors, the McKenzies were out of town, hence the reason why this information is not coming to light until now. We asked him if he remembered when it happened, and he said he thinks it was on his birthday, which means the day in question would have been September tenth of last year. He remembered going downstairs afterward for his parents to sing happy birthday to him. Several weeks later, when police were canvassing the area, there was a report that the Waldrops' daughter had been seen on the block. However, that was never corroborated.

"At least this gives us more to go on. We'll look at attendance records of the department to see who was on duty that day. Brian McKenzie also described the bad guys as wearing street clothes."

"Does he remember what they looked like?"

"Vaguely. He did say that one guy, the guy that was driving, was tall, like a basketball player. We've scheduled a second interview to talk to him further and show him some photos. Hopefully, he'll recognize some of the men he saw."

As Hill lay in his hospital bed, a breaking news report flashed on the ceiling-mounted TV in the room:

"A prominent attorney, Fred Rivers, who was a former prosecutor for the Hines County Municipal District, jumped to his death this morning from his thirty-second-floor condo at the Millennium Place condominium complex. Police are currently on the scene. Let's go to Dick Clayton for more on this story. Dick?"

"Hi, Michelle, details at this point are sketchy. However, what we *do* know is that this attorney, according to his family and colleagues, had been despondent recently over a pending divorce from his wife, and allegedly also suffered from depression, not only stemming from the divorce, but from the stress of his profession as well. Police aren't saying much at this point, only that there appears to be no foul play involved. Dick Clayton for KTIN News. Michelle, back to you."

Michelle Banter, KTIN News co-anchor, said: "This is the fourth attorney in Hines County to commit suicide this year, which is quite alarming, to say the least. And clearly a troublesome trend. You would think these attorneys had access to some type of support system to let them know there's help available when they need it. Such a shame."

Minutes later, while still processing the reported death of the attorney, Hill received an unexpected visitor. The woman who walked into the room had known about him, however, had lost contact once her sister died. She was there to deliver a startling revelation. He was wide awake, laying upright, still watching television when she walked in.

"Hi, John. You may not remember me. My name is Trudy Simmons. You dated my sister Erica a long time ago. You both worked at the same office building over on Pinecrest. Do you remember?"

"Yeah, I think I do. How are you?"

"Good, and I hope *you're* doing better."

"I'm doing okay under the circumstances. Your sister—how is she? She married now?"

"Unfortunately, she passed away several years ago from a prescription overdose. And there was no note left behind."

"Sheesh, I'm sorry to hear that. I was hoping for better news."

"Well, I do have some other news for you, and I'm not sure that this is the right time, or if it's ever the right time. But I've been keeping a secret and didn't know where to find you until I recognized your picture in the paper. I put two and two together and figured out you had been brought here, since this is the closest hospital to where the shooting occurred."

Hill, feeling anxious, beads of sweat dotting his forehead, wondered *why now?* Why, at this particular time, would he have to hear whatever this woman had to say?

"What I have to tell you, John, is that my sister had a baby—and she always said that you were the father."

Hill, looking flustered now, like a deer in the headlights, reached for the remote to mute the volume on the television.

"Erica had a baby girl and named her Jessica Kelly Hill."

"Why the hell didn't she tell me?" Hill asked.

"She was still in school at the time, only working part-time, and figured she'd had her whole life ahead of her. And to be honest, she just couldn't handle the responsibility. She didn't want you to have any input because she was adamant about giving the baby up for adoption. All she told me was that the baby was adopted by a nice family and had a better chance at succeeding in life compared to what she could offer that child."

"Not to sound like a jerk here, but are you sure she's my kid?"

"Erica was a hundred percent sure; she assured me that she hadn't been with anyone else. And Jessica, from what I remember, looks exactly like you."

"Do you know who the family is, or where they could be found?" asked Hill.

"No. I'm sorry, I don't. The only thing I can offer is that now that you know she exists, perhaps you could find her somehow. I would assume that she might already be in college by now. I'm sorry to have to tell you this after the fact, and under these circumstances, but I couldn't live with myself if I didn't, especially now that I could actually talk to you."

"I appreciate it. Don't feel too bad. I can't keep a secret either." He smiled while trying to push up higher, still wincing in agony from the gunshot wound. The pain medication was becoming less effective.

"I know they don't want visitors staying too long, so I'll let you rest. Here's my contact information." Simmons stood and leaned over to put a handwritten note on the food tray next to Hill's bed. "I hope you find her, and the two of you can have a relationship," she said.

"Thanks, Trudy. This obviously means the world to me. Had I known about her, I would have been there all along. She *has* to know this wasn't my fault."

"She will. Take care and be sure to keep in touch." Simmons smiled and patted the top of Hill's hand as she prepared to leave the room.

After she left, he lay there staring at the ceiling, feeling that the preceding ten minutes had been completely surreal. He still hadn't quite come to grips with it. *He had a daughter*, a child he knew nothing about. *Where was she? How old was she, and how would he find her?*

Now more than ever, he was determined to leave Hines County Hospital and find his daughter, hoping to experience fatherhood by having some type of bond with her. And since Hill's own father had died when Hill was young, he knew all too well what the effects of not having a parent present could be. This meant everything to him.

He quickly called his brother and family to tell them the news.

CHAPTER **12**

BASED ON THE evidence gathered during the investigation, Hines County Judge, Alfred Brunson, approved the execution of a search warrant for the premises located at 158 Mulholland Drive. This would be a joint effort, including multiple agencies. The FBI, DEA and a Major Crimes Unit Task Force were assembled for the early-morning raid. It was just before 5 a.m. on a Tuesday. Cold and damp. A slight morning fog crept through the predawn darkness.

A procession of high-tech law enforcement vehicles pulled onto Mulholland, unbeknownst to any of the residents in the neighborhood.

The vehicles parked in a synchronized fashion at the entrances of the property and around the perimeter. Each agent quickly exited his or her vehicle wearing Kevlar, with guns drawn, taking their positions while awaiting the go-ahead. FBI Agent Preston Ponder was in charge and knew the dangers of this operation all too well. He motioned a group of Lake Park Narcotics-Vice Unit investigators to position themselves at the front and back doors and around the perimeter. Two police canine unit officers pulled up in front of the house with search dogs, and jogged across the grassless lawn to assemble with the rest of the team.

Ponder slunk to the rear of the house and counted off into his Motorola talkie as the men readied to forcefully enter.

"Okay, guys, everyone take your positions. Let's do this on three. Here we go. One… two…"

Then suddenly, a homeless vagrant appeared out of nowhere, his face worn, his clothes tattered, his body strongly reeking of alcohol. He stumbled as he shouted a warning to the men: "Don't do it! It ain't worth it! You'll pay with your lives!" The man choked out a laugh and staggered backwards. His voice was hoarse and throaty from years of drinking.

"Get out of the damn way. Back up!" one of the agents whispered fiercely while waving him back.

"Okay, you assholes have been warned," the man mumbled as he was quickly taken into custody by extra officers on the scene.

"Guys, there was an interruption. Let's try this again," Ponder said. "One… two… three…"

Both the front and back doors of the house were leveled from the force of the battering rams, as the men filtered into each entrance of the dilapidated home. They saw no one. The agents continued their search, while aiming their weapons and ballistic shields forward, ready to respond with deadly force if necessary. They cautiously proceeded through the property, unprepared for the stench that hit them as soon as they came inside.

One of the men held a flashlight in his left hand while holding a Glock in his right. The light illuminated some strange markings on the wall.

"Look at this. What *is* that?" he said as the group peered at the red painted symbolism.

"That's a symbol used by satanic groups. These scumbags are *out* there, obviously into more than just committing crimes."

Then they proceeded down a hallway going from room to room, flipping light switches and checking closets with no success. There was no sign of anyone. "Come on, let's check these other rooms," Ponder ordered.

It was obvious that Crowley had been tipped off about the raid. The electricity had been completely shut off. There were no drugs, guns, dead bodies or any evidence of sex trafficking as intel had indicated. Then, Ponder recalled the secret meeting downtown, where it had been revealed that there was some type of subterranean operation beneath the house. Until now, he hadn't given the disclosure plausibility, since it had been hard for him to fathom at the time.

"Guys, supposedly there's an underground facility beneath the basement. They knew we were coming and moved everything out before we got here. We need to find the entrance to get below ground. Let's keep looking. Everyone downstairs—that's the logical place to start." All the men hurried to the basement, descending in a single line behind Ponder.

"I want every room, door, closet and any other spaces checked for openings." The men split up in groups going in opposite directions, each having to step in puddles of leaking water while avoiding spider webs hanging from the nine-foot ceiling. Nothing was found until a relative newcomer to the team named Eric Doyle came upon a sliver of light showing through from a crevice in the floor. Doyle was a hotshot cop from Detroit who had relocated to the area two years ago and moved quickly up the ranks, impressing his superiors with a penchant for getting things done, even though he didn't always play by the rules. He had been appointed team leader of this unit, much to the dismay of cops that had more tenure within the department.

"Guys, I think I've got something here," he whispered to those close by. The cops quickly huddled closer to take a look.

Doyle eased down to the ground to put his ear to the crevice. "I hear someone talking down there. It's got to be an opening somewhere." The men followed him as he began walking slowly, running his hands over the walls, trying to detect something that would indicate an opening. Suddenly, the men heard what sounded like footsteps coming up a set of stairs. They all took positions, ready to fire their weapons as a concealed door opened inside of a nearby utility closet. Out came a burly figure standing about six foot five with what looked like the width of a Mack truck.

"Police, hands in the air! Down on your knees, now!" the agents barked. The big man complied, slowly lowering himself to the cold concrete below.

"Who else is down there?" one of the agents asked.

"If you want to know, go look for yourself," the suspect scoffed in a foreign accent, a sarcastic smirk on his face. Three agents stood over him, their guns aimed at his torso, while one handcuffed him from behind and read him his Miranda rights.

The rest of the team started toward the lower level. While they descended a set of retractable steel stairs, the whole area went pitch black. Someone had shut off the lights, and the men, still on the stairs, suddenly knew this wasn't going to be easy.

Ponder quickly pulled out his Motorola and whispered, "We're going to need extra backup. I want the perimeter surrounded, and I need additional manpower with night vision equipment now!" There were no windows, and whoever was in the area had the advantage of knowing exactly where to hide. Ponder figured that the lower level either had a separate electric supply line or had to be powered by generators.

Minutes later, additional police personnel arrived with special night vision goggles the department had recently procured. It was commonplace for certain technology to find its way from being used exclusively in the military, to trickling down to law enforcement departments around the country.

The arriving agents quickly went inside to meet with Ponder and his team. Minutes later, after bringing everyone up to speed and donning the goggles, the men hurried through the area with automatic weapons pointed in all directions. Several of the agents came upon a steel door that was locked.

"Move back. I've got this," said Ponder as he used the butt of his assault rifle to remove the locked door handle. Then, with a quick step back, he kicked the door in. The agents rushed forward and were suddenly met with a spray of bullets as some of Crowley's henchmen waited inside for the right moment to attack. Bullet holes littered the entranceway and door frame. Lethal rounds penetrated flesh, severely injuring three agents during the exchange. The men clutched their wounds as blood flecked the concrete slab. Several of Crowley's men were also hit and seriously wounded as others attempted to cower behind wooden pallets containing heroin from Puerto Palomas, worth millions of dollars.

As the gun battle ceased, the injured men lay on the floor squirming in pain, surrounded by empty shell casings and the smell of gunfire.

Ponder then shouted, "Give up if you want out of this place alive! It's surrounded. Come out now... hands in the air!" Two of the perpetrators who were not injured threw down their weapons and slowly walked out from behind the wooden crates. Ponder and his team quickly apprehended the men, placing them in handcuffs. Ambulances were called to the scene to take the injured to Veteran's Legacy Memorial Hospital.

First responders went inside to tend to the wounded still lying on the floor. Ponder knelt over one of his fallen comrades while signaling for several EMTs to come over and take a look.

He was wrought with emotion while hoping for a positive outcome.

"Sir, I've checked for a pulse and any signs of life. I'm sorry to say, we lost him," one of the EMTs said as he glanced up at Ponder. Ponder's face turned blush red; his chest tightened, and he felt a lump in his throat. It was if someone had punched him in the gut and ripped his heart out. He felt responsible for the loss of any of his men. After all, they were under his command. He watched sadly, with an empty stare, as the body was removed and taken outside. He quickly followed.

There was still a lot of work to do and potential evidence to uncover. The local media received word of the raid and ensuing gun battle and descended onto Mulholland Drive in droves. As several men, including Ponder, emerged from the house with the offenders in cuffs, reporters sprang into action.

"Can you tell us if the suspects you have in custody are police officers, and if there is any connection between what happened here and Officer Mike Crowley?" one reporter asked. "Was anything found in the house that would indicate a criminal enterprise was indeed taking place here?" asked another.

Ponder stopped in his tracks to answer. "I can tell you that this investigation is just beginning, and so for that reason I cannot comment on any specifics at this time. What I *can* tell you is that there is a lot to process inside this house behind me, and as further details become available, we will make them known to you at the appropriate time."

Another reporter shot out a question, as if he were oblivious to everything that Ponder had just stated. "Sir, there's been speculation that this house has been a storage space for people that were murdered or had gone missing. Can you confirm if any of that is true?"

"Again, we don't have any details as of yet, and I'll have no further comment for now. Thank you."

"Gentlemen, please step back. We need this area clear to finish processing the scene," another officer shouted. Suddenly, Ponder was requested back inside. The rest of his team, still in the house, made a gruesome discovery. He quickly walked up the creaky steps into the house while looking at its deplorable condition, presuming that Crowley and company must have intentionally let the place deteriorate to keep it from drawing any unwanted attention. He walked through a hallway down to the basement, and into the lower level, where the others were waiting.

"Sir, we've got something here," Doyle said as he opened the door to a small room. Inside there was an Epson video projector mounted to the ceiling. Four women and a young girl who looked like she wasn't even out of high school lay on the floor with their hands behind their backs. All five of them were half-nude, bound and gagged, and all had been sickeningly starved. They were weak, and clearly in pain from the duct tape wound tight around their faces, hands and feet. Ponder was shocked at the deplorable condition that the women were in, presumably left for dead on the cold, damp concrete floor. The room had no windows, and the temperature could not have been more than forty degrees.

The men freed them, and as soon as the tape was removed, the women and the girl screamed and cried uncontrollably, hugging the agents, thankful for being found.

One of them looked extremely frail and malnourished to Ponder, like the woman had not eaten in days. There were bruises and markings on their torsos and necks from being collar-chained and beaten.

"Have you been down here long?" Ponder asked the woman.

"Yes," she said, her voice quivering, still trying to contain her emotions. "We've been held here captive, used as sex slaves and before that, prostitutes."

"Come with me, we're getting you out of here, *all of you,*" said Ponder. The agents took off their jackets to give them to cover the exposed parts of their bodies before leading them outside.

They followed the men up the stairs, through the basement and out of the house, past the officers assigned to cover the exits. Then they were escorted by EMTs, who helped them into several waiting ambulances. Ponder retreated back in the house to accompany the crime scene techs and the rest of the team inside.

One of the agents came running toward him. "We've got everything we were looking for sir, come this way." The two went back to the lower level, this time through a long corridor, wide enough to drive a small truck through.

"How long is this tunnel?" Ponder asked.

"We don't know just yet. We suspect it was used as a route of some sort, perhaps to smuggle drugs and/or weapons from point A to point B. Look in here—this is what we've found," said the agent, as the two entered what looked like some type of large storage area. The entire room was made from cinder block and painted a dark, utilitarian gray. There were no windows and no artificial or natural light. It looked more depressing than a maximum-security prison cell.

"So this is where Crowley and the rest of those scumbags hid everything. Have we looked inside those?" said Ponder, as he pointed toward several large metal bins locked with steel keypad entry. Elsewhere in the room were duffel bags full of the latest weapons of choice, including AR-15 assault rifles, stacks of sealed bags of heroin, cocaine, marijuana, and two Rubbermaid containers full of bags of ecstasy.

"Okay, let's round this stuff up, take it outside and get someone down here that can get these bins open," Ponder said. Doyle quickly put in the call. Crime scene techs were still all over the place, taking snapshots, dusting for prints and gathering physical evidence.

"They've got someone coming over, a welder, should be here in twenty minutes. And what the hell is this stuff?" Doyle asked as he held up what looked like some kind of bizarre Halloween costumes lying in a box in the corner. "Damn, not only are these guys criminals, it looks like they were having some type of satanic ritual here. Anybody see the movie *Eyes Wide Shut* with Tom Cruise?"

"Yeah, I saw that. It kind of creeped me out, except for Nicole Kidman of course."

"Well, I think that's what we're dealing with here. This is some real weird and freaky shit," Doyle said as he held up some type of purple plastic sex toy.

"Hey, make sure you've got gloves on when you touch that stuff."

"We just got word that the welding guy is here; they're bringing him down now."

"Where's the rest of the team?" Ponder asked.

"They're checking the rest of the area. I think they're preparing to see where the tunnel leads to."

"Tell the guys to stick together. Let's try to stay in one section at a time, to maintain safety."

"Will do," Doyle replied.

Two men entered the room. One was carrying a blowtorch, welding helmet, gloves and a bottle of butane. The welder, intrigued by the heavy police presence, quickly and nervously introduced himself.

"Hi, I'm Nick Daniels," he said.

"Pleased to meet you. Preston Ponder, FBI." The two men shook hands. "What we've got here, Nick, are these metal bins. And we need access to see what's inside. Think you'll be able to open them?"

Daniels rubbed his right hand over the smooth surface of one of the bins and gave it several knocks with his knuckles. "Let's see, looks to be pretty thick, but I can work around that lock area, should open right up."

"Okay, we'll get back and let you go at it," Ponder said. The agents padded back to a safe distance.

Daniels slipped on his helmet and lit his torch, making sure the heat was intense enough to melt the material. Sparks flew everywhere as he slowly moved the flame in a circular pattern around the lock area. Once finished, he stepped back, waving the smoke from around his face and lifting the helmet off his head.

"It should be good to go. Be careful, though. That whole area is still really hot. I've got a crowbar. Here, this should help," Daniels said.

Ponder grabbed the crowbar, hooked it onto the freshly cut section and tore it open. There was complete silence in the room as the agents stood, waiting intently. Once it was opened, the men were met with utter horror. The bin was filled from top to bottom with decomposed corpses wrapped in clear plastic body bags. Some had obviously been there longer than others. The cops stood there staring in disbelief, their hands and arms up to their noses to block the stench. Daniels turned away, not able to stomach the sight of what he'd just witnessed. Dead bodies were not something he was accustomed to seeing on job calls. Ponder and company had seen death before, but nothing of this magnitude up close. And never something *like this* in tranquil Lake Park.

The first thought that crossed his mind was that the bodies had been stored in the bins until a more permanent location could be found.

"Doyle, make the call," Ponder requested solemnly.

"Let's get these bodies out. I want the other bin opened, and every inch of this place searched. I want a crew of guys led by Doyle to go through that tunnel, on wheels if possible, to see where it leads to." Preston Ponder was more determined now than ever to bring down Crowley and his criminal enterprise, known as El Subida.

The assembled men entered the pitch-black tunnel on foot, with lights and firearms ready. It would have taken too long to get the proper type of vehicle in the area, and time was of the essence.

"Let's stay together and find out where this thing leads to," Doyle said. Each man's step followed the other as their boots hit the smooth surface of the floor in a synchronized fashion like soldiers marching into battle. Doyle was now in charge and had the respect of the rest of the team. An operation of this sort was something new even to him, and for the first time since relocating, he thought about his own mortality and the possibility that he might not make it home. This was his *job*, after all, what he was *paid* to do, and yet there was a part of him that relished the opportunity.

And so it began.

"Doyle, you see what I saw?" one of the cops asked.

"What?"

"There was some movement up ahead to the right."

"Alright, everyone proceed with caution," he whispered.

Each man moved forward alertly, with his finger wrapped around the trigger of his firearm. Their pace slowed, and their breathing became heavier. As they continued to trudge forward, they could still see some type of movement. It was a dark silhouette hiding in an opening. Whoever it was did not know the agents could see them.

"Come out! Hands in the air! Drop your weapons and get on the ground!" yelled Doyle. Suddenly, there was a loud, ear-splitting bang. The perpetrators bolted from the opening, and one pointed a Sig Sauer 9mm at the agents and squeezed off a volley of shots before he spun around to run down the tunnel. The agents, in fear for their lives, returned fire, striking one of the suspects several times in the back and watching him collapse onto the pavement. The other suspect disappeared in the darkness.

The sound of the gunfire was exceptionally loud, and fiercely echoed in the narrow, enclosed space. The men jogged to get a closer look, AR-15 rifles pointed at the subject in case he was still alive. Doyle kicked the handgun away from the body to one of the other agents as the men hovered over, processing what had just occurred.

The suspect lay there, immaculately dressed in a suit and tie. He was barely clutching a black Prada Saffiano leather attaché in his left hand.

"Should we open it?" one of the cops asked.

"Yeah, I think it's okay. He was trying to get away with it. It didn't look like he was trying to use the briefcase as a weapon. Let's see what's in here." Doyle knelt to the ground to open it, unlocking each clasp as he slowly raised the flap to see inside.

Inside there was a manila file folder, including some papers on top of tightly wound stacks of crisp hundred-dollar bills, as if they'd just left a bank. Doyle flipped through one of the stacks with his fingers, fanning the bills in the process.

"I'd say there's got to be at least twenty grand in here. Does this guy have any ID on him? Check his pockets," Doyle said as he continued to look through the compartments of the briefcase.

One of the agents reached into the dead man's front pockets, then back pockets, and found a leather Prada billfold wallet. He opened it and saw nothing.

"This guy's wallet is completely empty."

"Empty? You're kidding, right?"

"No, it's completely empty, look." The agent handed the wallet to Doyle for confirmation.

"Who the hell goes around with a completely empty wallet?"

"This guy's a criminal, so nothing they do surprises me. Let's look at those papers." The agent took the papers from the briefcase and handed them to Doyle for closer inspection.

"It says here: 'Payment to Gene & Elle Construction, Inc., for services rendered at the premises located at 158 Mulholland Drive,' and goes on to list the exact work that was done."

It became increasingly clear to Doyle that this was no ordinary, small-time criminal endeavor. These perps were being backed by people in high places, with major connections to pull off something of this magnitude, he thought.

"Upchak, Mitchell—see to it that they get this scumbag out of here. Brown and I will see how far this tunnel goes, or where it leads to. We'll meet you guys back on Mulholland."

Brown and Doyle walked the rest of the tunnel without incident, until they encountered a small set of stairs leading up to a door. They padded up the steps, opened the door and were temporarily blinded by fluorescent light from the area. The door was a passageway from the tunnel to an underground parking garage in a commercial district that was mostly inactive after midnight. It was a perfect location for Crowley and company to make entrances and exits without much fanfare.

Twenty minutes later, Brown and Doyle returned to the front of the property on Mulholland. Ponder was still helping to take evidence outside of the house and into a white-paneled police van parked along the side of the street. The two men walked toward Ponder to give him a report of what they saw.

"Sir, we went through to the end of the tunnel, and it leads to a set of stairs, which go up to a steel door that's locked from the other side, where there's an underground parking garage beneath Twelfth Street."

"How in hell did they build all this unnoticed? Anybody know?" Ponder asked.

"No, sir."

"Okay, let's wrap things up here. I think we've got everything. I've got a ton of paperwork that needs to be completed by tomorrow morning. This is going to be huge, gentlemen!"

"What's that?"

"For starters, solving this case. And I'm sure many others, once some of the bodies can be identified through DNA and dental records."

"What about Crowley?"

"What *about* him?"

"Well, what evidence do we have that links him to this?"

"We've got witnesses, some of which he's trying to dispose of. Unfortunately for him, his time's up. And that goes for anyone else involved. I'll see to it. There's a lot more work to do. I've got to put a report together and prepare for a press conference that we can expect in several days to answer questions about the latest in the investigation, including today's turn of events," Ponder said.

Major Crimes Task Force personnel returned from the raid, and the captured suspect was quickly ushered inside police headquarters and up to the interrogation room for questioning by detectives and the FBI, most of whom were salivating at the opportunity to squeeze information out of a member of *El Subida* and get incriminating details linking the organization's activities directly to Crowley.

Detectives sat down face to face with the suspect, his responses ready to be captured via the unassuming microphone and hidden camera in the room.

"Okay, douche bag, time to start talking. We want all the details about who's all involved, the who, what, when, where and how!"

"In five... four... three... two... one."

"I don't know nothing."

"Yes, you do."

"No, I don't," the suspect said belligerently with a grimace on his face.

"Okay, I'll tell you what. You're looking at ten to twenty easily, or possibly more depending on the additional charges. So, if I were you, in order to possibly help save my own ass, I'd start talking NOW! Start by telling us about the operation."

The suspect looked down and shook his head, then shoved back from the table in his chair.

"Can I get a drink of water?" he asked.

"Sure, somebody get him a drink of water."

"Look, man, that's one of the rules. *We don't snitch.*"

"Snitch? It's better *them* than *you*, right? If you want to take all the heat for them, go right ahead. Be my guest."

"Okay, okay, he's got distribution setups all over. He moves a lot of stuff to a lot of people—drugs, guns, women and young girls, whatever shit these people are into."

"Who is *he*, exactly?"

"Mike Crowley, man. That guy ain't wrapped too tight. I once saw him kill a man with his bare hands. I'll never forget that shit. He's crazy as hell, like he ain't got no fear in him.

None! Being a cop is just a front for him. All he cares about is dollars and cents."

"Who's his supplier?"

"I don't know. He never told us. He figured we'd make our own deals if we knew."

"So how do things get from point A to point B?"

The suspect paused for a beat. 'The tunnel. A *clever fucking idea* if I must say so."

"So everything is moved through the house?"

"Yeah, everything comes in from an undisclosed location, somewhere by some underground garage. That's all I know. So no one is ever really seen going in and out of the house, except, perhaps, Lake Park's finest." The suspect looked at the detectives and smiled. At that point he knew he was being a dick, and took pride in it.

"Tell us more about the tunnel and operation."

"All day long you hear movement, forklifts and small trucks moving things in and out. They move a lot of product to gangs and dealers up in Chicago, Milwaukee, Indiana, Detroit and Minneapolis."

"What else you got?" the detective asked.

"Murders, man. People have been killed there, never to be seen or heard from again, and those women and underage girls—they treat them like animals. They pimp 'em out to professional people, doctors, lawyers, judges, especially up in Chicago. Man… there are some sick fucks out there."

"So where's Crowley?"

"I dunno."

"Any guess?"

"Nah, he's a smart dude, though. I'll give him that. That dude is on the run. I think he's working with somebody inside, tipping him off."

The detectives looked at the suspect caustically.

"He *must* be. Why you think he's so hard to catch? All I know is, from the way the whole thing's set up, with all the high-tech shit they got, *somebody's* got their backs," the suspect said.

"So how much are they bringing in?"

"I ain't sure. I heard it's over a million, though."

"A year?"

"Nah… a month. All tax-free, of course. That's how they roll."

"El Subida?"

"Of course."

"Any links to friends across the border?"

"I already *told* you. I *don't know where* it comes from. Anyway, I've said enough. I wanna talk to a lawyer."

The detectives finished their interrogation and the suspect was placed in a holding cell.

The following morning an arrest warrant was issued for Mike Crowley. He had been officially off work for an extended leave of absence, and no one knew his whereabouts. Both local law enforcement and the FBI were looking to bring him in. It was not going to be easy. Crowley, being one of them, knew exactly what to expect and how to evade capture.

CHAPTER **13**

HILL WAS LOOKING forward to leaving the hospital, and my mother and I were thankful the outcome of the shooting was not worse. We had planned to check up on him when he suddenly called.

"John, how are you?"

"A lot better. Still in some pain, though. The doctor said I can go home tomorrow. I'll need to take it easy for a few days. But I can't go to my place. I'll be staying at my brother's house for the time being, and wanted to let you know."

"Have a way to get there?"

"Not really. My brother can't afford to miss work, and he and his wife only have one vehicle. So, I was wondering—"

"Listen, you don't have to ask. We'll be there for you. Just let me know what time."

"I'm thinking noon should be good, from what they've told me. And I have one other request, one other stop to make, if it's okay."

"Sure. Of course, we've got to be careful under the circumstances. It's obvious we've got targets on our backs. It's scary as hell to venture out now."

"I understand if you don't feel comfortable. That's okay, too. But I've got some interesting news to share with you. I got a visitor while here, who's the sister of a girl I used to date. Trudy Simmons is her name, and she told me that her sister had a baby girl, and that *I'm the father!* Imagine that!"

"Are you serious?"

"I am, and the baby was given up for adoption. So I'd like to go by the adoption agency downtown to see what other information I can find."

"That's amazing. Well, congratulations on being a dad! You've mentioned that you looked forward to being a father someday. What's her name? And do you know how old she is now?"

"Her name is Jessica, and I would imagine she's got to be in her late teens at this point."

"You're going to need as much information as possible to help you find her. It's a shame no one ever told you until now."

"Yeah, I know. Her mother was struggling with her own issues and wanted to handle things the way she saw fit, without any interference from me, or anyone else."

"We never know what surprises life has in store for us. How did this woman find you?"

"She said she'd recognized my name and picture in the paper, from the shooting. So much for privacy rights, huh?"

"I'm glad I can be of help. You've been such a friend to me and my mom. Wait, listen, I've got an incoming call from the hospital I need to take. I'll be there tomorrow at noon, or perhaps a little earlier."

"Thanks."

The next day I wheeled into the circular front entrance of Hines County Hospital to pick up Hill. My mother waited patiently in the vehicle as I clicked on the hazards before going inside.

"Hi, I'm here to pick up Mr. John Hill. He's being released today," I said to the information desk attendant. An older woman with white hair briefly searched the patient database.

"Okay, here's a pass. He's in room 203. Take those elevators up to the second floor and make a right."

"Thank you."

Hill gently hobbled out of the room as I approached.

"You made it. I'm ready, thanks for coming," he said.

"You're welcome. My mom's in the car. I'm going to drop her off at the hotel first before we head downtown, since it's on the way."

"No problem. You know, they offered to bring me down in a wheelchair, but I told them *no, gracias*. I wanted to do this on my own."

"Independent now, huh?"

"Got to be."

We entered the elevator and shuffled to the lobby to return the visitor's pass, then left. Thirty minutes later, we arrived at Lake Park's main adoption agency in the heart of downtown. There were a large number of people waiting to speak with only a handful of counselors. An older woman with glasses, a bad wig and an attitude instructed us to take a number and have a seat.

Forty-five minutes later, Hill's number was finally called. A tall, slender woman in a gray pantsuit and four-inch heels came from behind a metal desk with her hand extended.

"Hi, folks. My name is Marilyn Keating. How can I help you today?"

"My name is John Hill, and I'm here because I've recently found out that I have a biological daughter whom I knew nothing about, and I understand she's been adopted."

"Mr. Hill, do you have any proof that you're the biological father? A copy of a birth certificate, or any other legal documents?"

"No, I don't. I only have her name and place of birth."

"Do you know the name of the child's biological mother?"

"Yes, ma'am, the biological mother's name is Erica Simmons, and at the time she resided at 4511 Moyer Avenue in Lake Park."

Keating briefly looked down at her desk and took off her glasses to give Hill what figured to be some disappointing news.

"Okay, I'm limited in the amount of information that I can share with you due to state and federal privacy laws. I'm sure you can understand. However, I do see what looks like a match based on the information you've given. It also looks like her last name has been changed to her adoptive family's last name."

"And what is that?"

"Mr. Hill, I'm sure you're a wonderful guy and really want to locate your daughter. However, I've informed you that I can't disclose much personal information without you going through the proper channels. I'm sorry."

"Ms. Keating, I understand. But if you could simply give me a last name, then it will be up to me to learn more. I just want to find her. She probably doesn't even know I exist!"

"How did you know *she* existed?" Keating asked.

"Her mother, I'm told, passed away, and her mother's sister saw my picture in the paper, recognized me as the shooting victim and came into my hospital room to tell me about her."

"You're the guy who was shot in the drive-by that's linked to that whole police cover-up thing. I thought you looked somewhat familiar." Keating looked down again and took a deep breath, appearing sympathetic toward Hill and his cause, while apparently discarding any sense of accountability.

"Look, I could lose my job over this. But I've seen worse acts committed around this place. Here's what I'll do. I'll give you her adoptive last name, and that's it. That's the best I can do. You didn't hear it from me, alright?"

"Okay, you have my word."

"It's Waldrop. And that's all I can say for now, unfortunately. Good luck finding her."

"Jessica Kelly Waldrop. Thank you so much!" Hill said.

We left the adoption agency and ambled toward the parking lot. Hill's adrenaline was pumping at full capacity now. As soon as we climbed in the BMW, he reached in the backseat for his iPad, obviously still wincing in pain from the gunshot to his abdomen.

"You mind stopping by the Panera Bread down the street? We can grab something, and I can use their free Wi-Fi to find her."

I nodded. "Sure, not a problem. I hope you find her, and that she's still here. That would make things much easier."

"I knew my first order of business leaving the hospital would be to track down my daughter. I didn't have a clue where to start, but figured the local adoption services agency downtown would be as good a place to start as any. And I still have Trudy Simmons's number if I need additional information."

We parked the vehicle and put money in the closest meter for an hour and a half worth of time. As soon as Hill got in the restaurant, he angled for the nearest available booth while I stared at the menu and the assorted pastries, contemplating something to put down while here.

Hill quickly sat and logged on to the Internet. He Googled Jessica Kelly Waldrop and the words Hines County together to see what results were returned. There was plenty of information. The first article he read was about a Kelly

Waldrop who was a community volunteer for the local Boys and Girls Club of America, and there was another article about a Jessica Waldrop who had taken fifth place in the Hines County Annual Walk to End Hunger event.

"My heart is pounding in anticipation," Hill said anxiously. "Could one of these articles be about her? Could they both be about the same person? The only way I'll know for sure is to contact each organization to somehow get in touch with her," he went on.

I leaned over and noticed that neither article had a picture attached, and he still had no idea what she looked like. Still unsatisfied, he scrolled down further and clicked to go to the second page of search results. At the top of the page was a link to the story about the Waldrop family disappearance from their house on Mulholland. And the article made mention of the Waldrops' teenage daughter, Kelly Waldrop.

"All of a sudden, it all makes sense—the conversation I had with Rich, the realtor… and to think that if this *is* her, she might be presumed dead," he said and powered off his iPad. "I've got a burning desire to know for sure," he blurted and quickly pulled out his cell phone to call Marilyn Keating, the adoption counselor. He tapped the screen to put the phone on speaker.

"Ms. Keating, this is John Hill. I was there earlier today to find out about my biological daughter."

"Yes, I remember. How's your search going?"

"I'm glad you asked. I'm at a dead end here. I've come across numerous articles that could be about her, including the disappearance of a family bearing the same last name as hers, who lived at 152 Mulholland Drive. Please, *can you tell me if that was her address?*"

Keating paused, and the conversation went completely silent.

"Okay, because I feel sympathetic to your cause, yes, that's the address we have on file. I had no idea that the family had been missing. We were no longer in contact once she became of legal age. I feel bad for you and hope that you find the closure you're looking for. Let me know what else I can do to help. I've already put my job in jeopardy. So once again, you didn't hear this from me."

"I appreciate it, and I won't tell a soul!"

CHAPTER 14

THE ANXIOUSLY AWAITED press conference was finally about to take place in the Lake Park Police Department press room at headquarters on Fifth Avenue downtown. Reporters had arrived from around the country, and outside; the street was filled with satellite trucks, cameramen and curious onlookers, hoping to catch a glimpse of the city's dignitaries, including the mayor.

Inside the building was complete chaos as reporters from different news affiliates jockeyed for a position close to the podium to hear what the chief of police and mayor had to say about the investigation, which was now being called the Lake Park Shakedown.

A man in an oxford shirt and V-neck sweater walked toward the podium to greet the media and begin moderation.

"Good afternoon, ladies and gentlemen. My name is Josh Radcliff, and I am the assistant to Mayor Ted Armstrong. This evening's press conference will shed new light on the case at hand and will be followed by a Q&A period afterward. With that being said, I'll turn things over to the mayor."

Armstrong made his way to the platform, shaking hands with his assistant and the chief of police, George Hilbricki. Armstrong had been the mayor for over twenty years, and was affectionately known as the People's Choice Mayor, but now this scandal within the police ranks threatened to taint his otherwise pristine political image.

Election time was also approaching, and the residents of Lake Park demanded answers.

"Good day, everyone. For those of you not familiar with me, my name is Ted Armstrong, and I am the mayor of this great city. As some of you are aware, my office and staff are cooperating jointly with the U.S. Attorney's Office, the State's Attorney's Office, the Office of Professional Standards, the DEA and the FBI. We've already spent a considerable amount of time and money on this investigation. However, it is money well spent, as we here in Lake Park pride ourselves on fairness, honesty, and transparency, and we're not going to allow a select few with their own agenda undermine the integrity of this great city of ours. With that, I'm going to turn it over to George Hilbricki. Please hold any questions that you may have until the end of today's conference." Armstrong signaled to Hilbricki to come up to the podium.

Hilbricki stood from his seat, wearing a distinctive navy-blue police uniform, the left side of his jacket decorated with brass ornamentation indicative of his accomplished career, and calmly walked to the podium.

"Hello, my name is George Hilbricki and I am the chief of police of Lake Park, Illinois. Just to give you a little background about myself, I took over this department three years ago. I come from a family of police officers, including my father, who retired some time ago, and my grandfather, who was a precinct captain in Indiana. I'd also like to take this moment to thank the mayor, once again, for the confidence he has instilled in me. When I took this position, I made it perfectly clear that any rogue behavior by cops, or anyone else for that matter, would not be tolerated. I've been involved in law enforcement for over thirty-two years now and figured I'd seen it all, but the degree of depravity alleged to have occurred in this case has utterly shocked me to the core." Several journalists in the room gasped at Hilbricki's candid remark.

"That being said, here's what we know so far with regards to this case. You might want to listen carefully because I've got to go through quite a bit here." Hilbricki pulled his glasses from his pocket to read the notes on the podium.

"As we speak, arrest warrants have been issued for the following individuals: Mike Crowley, Phil Slauson, Nathan Roberts, Darryl Washington, Lawrence Ito, Rico Alcazar, and Derek Sparks.

"We have strong indications that these individuals were involved in, and are all implicated in, various crimes related to the investigation of the following. A criminal enterprise known as El Subida, which operated from an underground facility located at 158 Mulholland Drive. From what we gather, the phrase: *El Subida* means for 'the rise' or 'to rise up' in Spanish.

"The perpetrators' alleged crimes include, but are not limited to: the kidnapping and disappearance of the Waldrop family from the residence at 152 Mulholland Drive; the murder of media executive Bruce Massey; the attempted murder of John Hill; the brutal beating and sexual assault of Alexis Fields; the kidnapping and assault of her mother, Ms. Doris Fields; breaking and entering, trespassing and damage to city property; witness intimidation and tampering; drug trafficking sales and distribution; the illegal import and sale of firearms; sex trafficking, prostitution, and gross sexual imposition; felonious assault; and, last but not least, official misconduct.

"The house on Mulholland has become an abode of wickedness. As part of an organized crime contingent, these suspects have engaged in everything from murder and sex trafficking, to supplying drugs and guns to gangs in Chicago, and prostitutes and black-market prescription drugs to the city's elite. During the raid, our agents saw evidence of satanic rituals that included members of local government, including symbolism, paraphernalia and video tapes of the group's activities locked away in a secret vault. Some of the agents even commented that in their entire career, they had never investigated crimes of such a heinous nature as was discovered in that house.

"And sadly, we've just received word a few hours ago that the bodies of Richard and Nancy Waldrop are believed to be among those recently discovered underneath the house at 158 Mulholland Drive. I want to make it clear that this *has not yet been confirmed;* we're still awaiting forensic results and the completion of DNA testing, both of which is going to take additional time. Lastly, we're also looking into whether foul play was involved in the death of Fred Rivers, the Hines County prosecutor who fell to his death from his condo in Bradford Estates. We've since obtained credible information that El Subida has been targeting prosecutors who refused to accept payoffs, and who were instrumental in seeking convictions of key members of the organization. This investigation is ongoing. We expect more charges soon and will update everyone accordingly. Thank you."

Reporters hurriedly asked their questions, and Hilbricki fired back answers, even as his face showed signs of stress. But the looming question that had been on everyone's mind throughout the evening was: where was Crowley?

CHAPTER 15

JOHN HILL CONTINUED his quest to locate his daughter Jessica, and made a call to one of his contacts who was heavily involved in the case. This was his strongest lead yet, and he had hoped for a positive outcome under the circumstances. He scheduled an appointment for the following day to see Dave Warren, the Lake Park PD detective he'd met earlier in the investigation.

Hill didn't know much about Warren. But he believed the cop could be trusted, and whatever information that Warren could provide was information that he would not have known otherwise.

The meeting was scheduled for 9:30 a.m., and Hill pulled up to the 2nd District police station in a blue Ford Fusion SE which he had rented while his Ford Explorer was being repaired. He entered the building, walked to the front desk and informed a seated female cop of his appointment.

"Hi, I'm John Hill, and I have a nine thirty appointment to see Detective Warren."

"Okay, Mr. Hill, you can wait there. I'll call his office to let him know you're here." The woman pressed some buttons on her desk phone to notify Warren as Hill stood there, glancing at law enforcement personnel passing by; some bringing handcuffed arrestees into the building. There was a woman across the hall involved with a verbal confrontation with several officers, poetically peppering them with the type of language that would make a sailor cringe.

Warren eventually came walking down the hall to greet Hill. There was no smile on his face, only a stern look as he extended his hand for a shake.

"Mr. Hill, good to see you. Let's go into my office."

Both men started down the corridor, peering at the officers and the woman, still in attack mode.

"Just another day at the office," Warren joked in reference to the situation.

"Have a seat. Coffee?"

"No, thanks. I'm wired enough these days," said Hill.

"Yeah, I know the feeling. It's never a dull moment in this place. Five more years and I'm off to Myrtle Beach for my retirement."

"Looking forward to it?"

"No doubt about it. Great weather, beaches, and golfing. What exactly did you want to talk about today?" Warren asked.

"Well, to make a long story short, I recently found out that I have a biological daughter whom I knew nothing about."

"Congratulations, I guess that's a good thing," Warren said and chuckled.

"It *is* a good thing. The problem is, I've been trying to locate her, and now understand that she was adopted by the Waldrop family, who disappeared from 152 Mulholland. And I'm sure you're aware that the parents were found murdered at the house next door, in the basement, or whatever that underground area is."

"Wait, I may have something of interest to you." Warren rose out of his office chair, walked to a file cabinet, and pulled opened the bottom drawer. Then he removed a manila folder, sat down, and opened it as he leaned back in his chair.

"The Waldrops' daughter was being kept against her will in that house, but was rescued during the recent raid. Says here her name is Jessica K. Waldrop. Is that her?"

"Yes, thank God! That's her!"

"So *your* biological daughter is Jessica K. Waldrop?"

"Yeah, unbelievable, isn't it? How can I get in touch with her, Detective?"

"Well, according to my file, she's staying at one of the hotels near downtown, where she'll be residing temporarily. She's also been given an assumed name, and has been told to keep in contact with certain key players in law enforcement. I'm sure she'll be called to testify once this thing goes to trial. Here's what I'll do. If you'd like, I can try to arrange a meeting between the both of you here at my office, and we'll see how things go from there, but only *if* she's interested. That's the best I can do. I'm restricted on what I can share. Let me know when you're available, and I'll set something up. Fair enough?"

"Totally! How about ten a.m. tomorrow?"

Warren chuckled. "That's short notice, but I'll give it a shot. Let me confirm the day and time, and I'll let you know as soon as I talk to her."

Both men stood on their feet and shook hands, as Warren escorted Hill out of the room and walked him down to the parking lot. To Hill, this whole experience had been surreal, and the next twenty-four hours would seem like the longest of his life.

The call finally came in from Warren around 7:30 p.m. It was confirmation that Jessica would be there. Between the lingering pain from his injuries and the anticipation of finally meeting his daughter, he could barely sleep.

The following morning could not come soon enough. Heading toward the 2nd District police station, Hill sped through side streets to avoid the last of rush-hour traffic. After arriving, he parked his car, this time in the visitors' lot, before going in a side entrance and up to Warren's office. It was a little-known-to-the-public shortcut the detective had shown him the day before.

This was it.

Hill opened the door and glared right at her. He knew, without question, there was no way this could *not* be his daughter. The resemblance was definitely there. She stood up to greet him.

"Hi, Jessica. I'm John Hill, your biological father."

Warren kindly interrupted, "Listen, I have a quick meeting to go to downstairs. You guys can stay here as long as you like. Just be sure to keep the door shut completely. We've got some nosy folks around here," he said as he excused himself for the special occasion.

"Okay, will do," said Hill.

"Wow, I'm... I don't know what to say," Jessica said.

The two embraced as the tears welled up.

"You don't have to say anything. I would have been there for you all along, had *I known* about you."

"Even though the Waldrops treated me as their own, all this time, I've wondered who my real parents were," she said as she wiped streaming tears from her cheeks.

"I'm here for you always, and thank God you're okay now."

Hill placed a kiss on her forehead as they sat down to talk.

"That place was the absolute worst; I mean, a real house of horrors, and I hope they catch them all. Unless someone was in *my* shoes, trapped in that godforsaken hellhole, no one would have a clue about what it was like, the torture and beatings, the murders, the children, and the smell throughout. It was awful," she said.

"Children?" Hill asked.

"Yes, they would take us all into a pitch-black room to sleep in, and you could hear the children crying their hearts out at night. They were being held until they could be sold. I would often overhear them talking about the sick, twisted people who were looking forward to it." Jessica slowly glanced down at the floor to reflect, her emotions starting to get the best of her. "I don't know how many of them survived. I'm just so thankful that I did! And I miss Richard and Nancy so much."

"I was really sorry to hear what happened to the Waldrops. *Everyone* will be glad when this is over. And hopefully that house will be demolished, to help bring some type of closure to all affected."

"What was my mom like?" Jessica asked, her eyes bright with curiosity.

"Your mom was a good person… really. I know it may be hard for you to understand. But I think she just didn't know how to handle being a mother at such a young age, and I believe she really thought she made the best decision at the time, not only for her, but for you as well. I met your mom's sister recently, and that's how I found out about you. I'll introduce you to her."

Hill told her about his side of the family, about Alexis, how he would introduce them, and how Alexis was involved in the case, including being the current owner of 152 Mulholland. He warned Jessica about keeping a low profile, at least until the case was over. Crowley was still on the loose, and anyone who could help put him away had been marked for death.

Warren came back to the office and knocked on the door.

"Okay if I come in?" he asked.

"Sure. We appreciate you helping to bring us together, Detective. I'm forever grateful," said Hill.

"Hey, don't mention it. There's still some of us good cops around."

Hill asked if it was okay to take Jessica back to her hotel room at the Holiday Inn, where she would stay holed up until the case and trial were over.

Warren gave his approval on the condition that Jessica assented.

And she did.

They drove through the city, in no particular hurry, as Hill turned on some music via the Ford Fusion's SiriusXM radio signal.

Eventually, they arrived at the front entrance of the hotel and exchanged contact information. Hill waited with the motor running until Jessica got safely inside. He wondered if not telling her about him being shot in the drive-by was the right thing to do. He figured that she'd been through enough trauma, and didn't want to unnerve her any further.

Time was running short, and the feds were getting impatient. The authorities were looking for Crowley to bring him in for questioning. It was just a formality at this point. The feds had already anticipated his downfall, and the sooner it occurred the better.

There were no signs of him at his home, his workplace, or the house on Mulholland. He knew they were on to him, with all parties now engaged in a high-stakes game of cat and mouse. What authorities *didn't* know was that Slauson, the inside snitch, had been keeping Crowley in the loop.

The feds knew that getting to an experienced cop like Crowley, fast, was paramount. It was anyone's guess where he could go if apprehending him took too long. And he was well aware, that getting to key witnesses before the prosecution could put them on the stand greatly increased his chances of an acquittal.

CHAPTER 16

THERE WAS PLENTY of communication going around between the witnesses, the feds and the State's Attorney's Office. It was a priority that everyone involved stay informed. Hill spent the rest of the day at the hospital for follow-up treatment. The doctors, in their effort to give the best care available, wanted certainty that his wounds were properly healing.

The staff grew fond of him, and word soon spread among nurses and doctors that he'd met his daughter for the first time.

"Mr. Hill, we'll see you back in two weeks. Everything is healing as expected thus far. Continue taking your medication as directed, and let us know if you experience any discomfort between now and your next appointment."

"Okay, Doctor. Glad to know things are moving along!"

Hill stood up, left the room and walked out of the hospital into the breezy fall air. He had been here so long it was dark now.

He strolled to the patients' parking garage and scanned the lot. He didn't see his car, so he pressed the Horn button on the keyless remote to locate it. He remembered putting his duffel bag in the trunk, but now he wanted the bag on the passenger seat for easy access to some snacks he had stashed away for later.

As he bent over to pull the bag from the trunk, he was suddenly sucker-punched in the head from behind with a pistol. He collapsed. His blurred vision allowed only a vague snapshot of the attacker, who was still standing over him, wearing a ski mask. His limp body was hurled into the trunk, and the mugger sifted through his pockets and grabbed his cell phone.

The trunk was closed, and Hill was involuntarily put to sleep.

Within ten minutes, a text was sent to both Alexis Fields and Hill's daughter, Jessica, which read:

I've got an emergency and need you to meet me at Route 50 and Nightingale Road. Come quickly please!!!

Both Jessica and Alexis tried calling Hill regarding the disturbing text, but each of their calls went straight to voice mail. Jessica had just enough money to pay for a cab to take her to the location. Alexis quickly left her hotel room against her mother's wishes and got into her car to meet Hill. After all, he had been there for her through everything, she thought.

Jessica arrived there first and instructed the cab driver to pull up behind the blue Ford Fusion sitting on the shoulder of the road. She paid the fare, thanked the driver and informed him he could leave. Alone, in an increased state of panic, she approached the driver's side of the car, fervently looking for her father. Suddenly the door swung open; the occupant jumped out, punched her in the face, shoved her into the backseat and bound her mouth, hands and feet with duct tape.

Two down… one to go. This was getting easy, he thought.

CHAPTER **17**

IT WAS AROUND 7:30 p.m. when I pulled up facing the headlights of Hill's car. I killed the engine, but hesitated before exiting my SUV. It was odd not seeing John around anywhere. *Is it safe?* I wondered. *Take a closer look?* I climbed out of my X5 and walked toward the still-running Ford Fusion. I approached the driver's-side door to peer inside. As my face drew near the glass, the door suddenly flung open, slamming me to the ground. The attacker, in a crazed state of hysteria, jumped out swinging wildly as he stood over me, punching me several times in the face before he shoved me into the backseat on top of Jessica. As I lay dazed, almost incoherent, he used whatever duct tape he'd had left from her to bind my mouth, hands and feet.

Jessica and I moaned and squirmed in a hair-raising pulse of terror, totally unknowing of what could come next. The attacker climbed into the driver's seat, dropped the accelerator and gunned it down Route 50, cutting a sharp right onto an unpaved road. The back tires screeched, kicking up gravel and debris from the thunderous rate of speed the car was going.

He must have known the area well, known exactly where he wanted to go next. There were loud thumping sounds emerging from the trunk, as if something was being tossed about like a rag doll.

Jessica and I desperately looked to escape from this hellish death ride. I glanced down and noticed that she'd been able to wrench the tape from her wrists, which in turn allowed her to do the same for me. Once free, we smartly continued to moan and sway, in an effort to make the maniac think we were still bound.

Then, as if on cue, we both rose and grabbed the son of a bitch from behind, pummeling and choking him as he tried to fight us off with one hand while clasping the steering wheel with the other. The vehicle swerved onto an embankment. The attacker lost control, and the excessive rate of speed caused the Ford Fusion to veer before slamming into a guard rail, dangling halfway over a cliff, overlooking a tree-filled ravine about 600 feet below. The attacker, still slumped over the steering wheel, groaned, appearing to be seriously injured from the impact.

We feared dying a horrible death as the car teetered. My pulse racing, I carefully leaned forward and grabbed his gun from the front passenger seat. Suddenly, there were cries for help coming from the trunk. We climbed out, removed the keys from the ignition, then pressed the Trunk button on the keyless remote to open it and were astounded to see it was Hill. We helped him from the trunk just as the attacker started to come to. He removed his ski mask, managed to twist his body around and was glaring at the three of us out of the rear window.

"I should have killed you when I had the chance, you snobbish bitch!" he screamed from the driver's seat, blood streaming from the side of his face, his voice horridly reverberating through the open space of the expanse.

"Guess what, Crowley, YOUR TIME'S UP, ASSHOLE!" I shouted as I feverishly pointed the gun toward his body and fired off shot after shot through the glass of the car's rear window. The barrage of bullets sliced into his torso and the driver's seat, igniting a force of motion that caused the Fusion to inch closer over the edge. Suddenly there was a loud, piercing snap, and the vehicle jerked forward, catapulting over the cliff, striking several gargantuan trees before crashing down into the brush-filled ravine below.

After several minutes, we cautiously walked toward the edge and stared at the vehicle as it lay upside down. Moments later, it burst into flames, shooting fiberglass, metal, and body parts high in the air. I took a deep breath and a sigh of relief. *It was finally over...* I thought.

Suddenly, walking toward us from a distance, a shadowy figure emerged. The first thought that came to mind was that it was an innocent bystander offering help.

But it wasn't.

As the man approached through the darkness, I recognized him instantly.

"Dr. Khan, what brings you here?"

"I was looking for Officer Mike Crowley. I was hoping that I could find him here," he said.

"He's dead."

"How?"

"He abducted John, and tried to kidnap John's daughter, Jessica, and me so that we couldn't testify against him. We struggled with him in the car and managed to escape and shoot him. He then went careening over the cliff. He wasn't at all who he appeared to be. And in his attempt to kill us to save himself, he died."

"How unfortunate. For *him*, that is. However, it's a good thing to know... *that* part is taken care of," Khan said.

"What do you mean?" I asked.

Khan chuckled, pulling a large metal handgun from inside his cashmere coat and aiming it toward the ground.

"You think you're so fucking smart, don't you? Well, you don't know the half of it. There were a lot of people looking for Crowley, and not just the FBI or police, mind you. *Well-connected and powerful people!* People who had a vested interest in him and his operation. But he started to get sloppy, out of control, assaulting you and bringing a lot of unwanted attention to himself and his activities. So the first order of business was to implant him with a small tracking device, a transponder, so we could monitor his whereabouts, in case he tried to run off with all the good stuff once everything started to unravel.

"That's how I knew to find him here. It was part of a larger project that I've been working on. The future of technology is here, *now!* The implant can be easily inserted during certain procedures via a syringe, without the subject even knowing. Although some of them later complained of acute pain at the point of entry, most likely from the body's immune system rejecting the device.

"Crowley had to come to the ER after a purposely orchestrated accident. That's when I embedded it. He *had* to be found before the feds found him. He *knew* too much!"

My heart started to hammer wildly while listening to this asshole, coming to the stark realization that he had implanted the device in me as well.

"You planted that thing in me?!" I said furiously.

Khan retorted, "We could have made something special together, you and I, if you weren't so fucking standoffish. Well, it's too damned late for that now! Of course, I can't let you or your friends walk away from here alive. So, that being said, this will have to conclude our meeting for tonight." Khan slowly raised his gun and pointed it in Hill's direction. Still hiding the semiautomatic I'd retrieved from Crowley, I quickly pulled the weapon from behind my back and aimed it at Khan, shooting him twice in the chest with the remaining two bullets left in the gun.

Khan fell backwards, collapsing onto the cold, damp pavement. Crimson blood oozed from between the sides of his coat as he gasped his last breath. Jessica, Hill and I hugged each other intensely, as Khan's lifeless body lay on the ground.

Our bond was sealed forever.

In Alex Dean's most terrifying novel yet,
the drama continues as Alexis Fields seeks to leave
the harrowing past she left behind, but finds herself
in the throes of a sadistic psychopath ...

Please turn this page
for an exciting peek at

Stalked.

MY EYES FLEW open to the sound of something or someone inside my condo as I lay asleep. Terrified, I began quietly easing upwards, my pulse hammering, back pressing against the headboard of the bed.

I immediately conjured thoughts of the torment and the harrowing past I so desperately wanted to leave behind. Something in my chest started to flutter. My eyes were wild as panic bloomed in the pit of my stomach.

Nervously peering across the room, I could now see a dark shape, smoothly and silently slinking about the doorway. Slowly. Moving closer—toward me. It was definitely moving, whatever it was, *whoever it was.*

Closer.

I lay there, paralyzed in terror as *it* crept closer. *Oh, God, no! This can't be happening!*

My heart raced as the masked intruder suddenly and swiftly lunged forward and violently grabbed me by my throat, pulling me out of bed as I tumbled onto the floor.

I screamed at the top of my lungs and tried to regain my balance as he held me down, one of his hands tightly gripping me like a horse's collar, the other pulling my hair back—commanding me to look up at him in horror.

My arms and legs flailing, I frantically stretched and grabbed the porcelain lamp from my nightstand, then managed with all of my adrenaline-fueled strength to swing, smashing it into his face.

The blow stunned him. He grunted and wavered momentarily. It was enough to allow me to free myself and run for the door of my condo to escape.

I unlocked the dead bolt and wrenched the handle, then darted into the hallway. I could hear him following close behind. I'd been able to move fast enough to get out before he leaped in a desperate attempt to stop me cold.

"HELP!! PLEASE!! SOMEBODY HELP ME!!" I screamed down the hallway, banging my fist on several doors as I ran toward the emergency exit stairwell.

I looked back and saw that he was still behind me. His face was hideously covered with some type of streaked silicone mask. He was dressed all in black. *Who the hell was this and why was he after me?*

I ran down the concrete stairs and hobbled out into the building's underground parking garage, panting, looking around for my car, for somebody, anybody to help me.

I bolted to Section C, the area where I last remembered parking.

I surveyed my surroundings, shaking, gripped in panic as I tried to get one of my car's doors open. *Dammit!* No keys. My eyes pinballed across the area. He was gone now. Vanished. Had he stopped chasing me? Could I have lost him somehow?

I felt a sense of relief as I crumpled down onto the cold concrete of the parking garage and nestled my back against the driver's side door of my BMW.

I closed my eyes for a split second to calm my frazzled nerves, wishing my pulse would simmer down. I took in a deep breath, silently wondering just what the hell was happening here. Was this all a bad dream?

Suddenly, I heard the patter of footsteps fast approaching, widely opening my eyes in fear.

I sat horrified and in shock as this monster stood before me with a sapphire-colored motorcycle helmet in his right hand.

Before a scream could escape my body, he abruptly lunged forward and furiously swung the helmet, aiming it directly at my skull—delivering a thundering *WHACK!*

My head snapped sideways, the bone-crushing blow rendering me senseless as I collapsed to the pavement.

I came to with blurred vision, a throbbing ache at the top left side of my head, and what looked like at least six human figures standing around me, staring as I lay semiconscious.

"Alexis? Alexis, can you hear me?" a woman in light blue scrubs inquired.

"Where… where am I?" I managed groggily.

"You were found unconscious in the parking lot of your building by a passerby. Somehow you suffered a serious injury to your forehead. A bleeding wound. Only God knows how you got there. Do you remember anything? Do you know what happened to you?"

"I… I vaguely remember running."

"What were you running from?"

"Running down the hall… from my condo," I murmured.

"Alexis, I'm Dr. Norvesh Patael," said a short, heavily accented man with a stethoscope, inching closer to the side of the bed. "We'd like to know who or what exactly were you running from?"

"Someone was chasing me. He... had a mask. I ran to the parking lot. That's... that's all I can remember," I slurred slowly.

"You're very fortunate your injuries were not more severe. You're suffering from cerebral edema. There is quite a bit of swelling in some of your brain tissue, along with some nasty-looking lacerations on the side of your head and the soles of your feet. I've scheduled an MRI for you first thing in the morning. We'll be monitoring you and running more tests to rule out any other complications. All things considered, I think your prognosis will be okay."

"Thank you, Doctor," I managed in a whisper.

"You're going to need some time off work, and the police will want to interview you to find out just what the hell happened."

A short and stocky nurse standing by quickly chimed in. "Alexis, I'm Frieda, the assistant on duty, and I'll be looking after you. Don't hesitate to alert me if you need help. We'll let you get some much-needed rest. Dr. Patael will be ordering more tests in the morning."

"Thank you," I replied as my eyes worked hard to stay open. Attentively, I watched each of them leave the room before nodding off into a deep slumber.

I tossed and turned, then awoke from what seemed like a terrifying nightmare around 3:30 a.m. My breathing was quick and labored. My skin was perspiring excessively.

I could still feel my attacker's hand around my neck. I'd envisioned him standing over me, this time naked, wearing that ghoulish Hollywood fright mask and holding what looked like a twelve-inch knife in his right hand.

Was it real? Had I been dreaming?

I could no longer sleep and quickly craned my neck toward the partially drape-covered window, yearning for a breath of fresh air.

I calmly lay there and took in a deep breath as I imagined the sights and sounds of Michigan Avenue. Shimmering street lights flickered in the darkness.

So much horrific violence and death struck the city every day, especially on the south and west sides, and now, here I lay, once again—a defenseless victim myself.

However, Chicago, with its gorgeous lakeshore, its vibrant nightlife and Magnificent Mile shopping, was still a beautiful place to be.

So... so beautiful, I thought... until Nurse Frieda was contacted by the Chicago police in an effort to interview me. They told her that Wilfred, my ex, might have been seen in the area.

How on earth could he have known I was here? And more importantly, *Does he know where I live?* He has promised to make my life a living hell.

I continued recoiling from the evil threat he had blurted the day he'd held that razor-edged knife to my throat. "*It ain't over*" still resonated in my head, leading me to believe it was true.

As my pulse raced.

Wednesday 8:40 A.M.

SARAH STALWORTH'S HANDS shook while she applied her mascara, eyeliner and lipstick as she readied for work as a communications specialist for a downtown transportation logistics firm.

She had managed to find stable employment in the River North area establishment, located in the trendy area just outside of Chicago's Loop. She would telecommute and did not have to appear at the office in person.

She worked alone from her near-North Side apartment, and only a low-resolution image of her face was visible over the company's network when she corresponded with other employees and clients of the firm.

This was almost perfect, she thought. She considered it one of the perks of the job. Priceless. Anonymity was key.

Today was going to be a new beginning, a renaissance of sorts in her sick and twisted mind. Work was not the real focus here. No, the real focus was murder. Simple, yet perfectly planned and executed, murder.

Some absolutely worthless, unsuspecting female victim, Stalworth thought. Not just anyone, mind you. One who would fit the necessary profile. One who would demand extraordinary attention from the media and police.

One who would make Sarah Stalworth Chicago's version of the Grim Sleeper Killer, only in a shorter amount of time.

She paced endlessly around her apartment before taking a seat in front of the widescreen all-in-one sitting atop the black corner desk in the living room. She calmly grabbed a nearby cup of cheap decaf, emptied two packs of sugar into it, and logged on to the internet.

Her background had been specific to computer programming, but she had accepted her current position with the understanding that she would be transitioned into a programming-oriented job once one became available.

She had not taken the time to do much in the way of socializing, but she expected that to change soon. The majority of her time had been spent surveying Chicago's dating scene, where she would engage her first victim.

Horny men who worked at the logistics firm found her attractive, in an odd and kinky kind of way.

They quickly became captivated with the new hire, seen only over their twenty-one-inch monitors. That seductive voice of hers, which sounded like one you'd hear on a phone sex line, was quite the turn-on, they thought.

They would send her suggestive personal messages frequently. But Sarah wasn't interested in them. She often spurned their awkward advances while keeping her preference for women a secret.

After she'd drained the disgusting cup of decaf, she logged in to an erotic chatroom she had visited often, eager to meet another woman for a one-night stand of carnal passion.

A small light hovered just above her avatar and indicated that she was online now.

"Hey, I like your profile and your picture, even though it's kind of blurry," said a young and attractive chatroom participant.

"Why, thank you! I like yours too!" Stalworth replied.

"Sooo many people don't post their real pictures. So, I just have to ask. Is that your real picture?"

"Of course. Don't be silly. That's why it's blurred. I can't risk being seen by people at my job. Even though they're all a bunch of perverts!"

"LOL. I know, right? You're funny."

"Freaks and perverts are everywhere. We have to choose our poison, I say."

"So what are you into? I can't tell much from your profile. There's not much to it. You like BDSM, or are you just into plain vanilla sex?"

"I'm open to trying anything. The naughtier and kinkier the better. It's all more satisfying that way. And I live for the thrill of it! What *is* life without adventure?"

"LOL! You certainly have an interesting way with words. I can't wait to meet you!"

"Ditto."

"Well, talking over the internet is safe, but *so* limiting. At least I think so, anyway. My friends all tell me that I need to stop being so rigid and live on the edge sometimes. That being said, I'm free tonight. Are you up to meeting at a public place to continue?"

"I sure am. And I was actually thinking the same thing. How about the Big Bowl on Ontario? I don't know how far you are from me now, but it's convenient, downtown."

"Okay. What time?"

"8:00 p.m. works for me."

"Sounds good, I'll meet you there at eight. I'll have on a faded denim outfit."

"Okay, cool."

Stalworth left her apartment, drove several miles over to Wells Street, parked in a nearby garage, and met young Taylor Hagenstock in the dimly lit restaurant in the heart of River North. The woman was cute in a schoolgirlish way, brunette, average height with a thin build.

The two hit it off and conversed at length, sipping pomegranate cocktails at the bar in between brief exchanges about each other's backgrounds.

Casual chitchat had become a precursor, a formality in such encounters before moving on to doing what they had both come to do.

A hostess promptly seated them in the dining room and they waited for a server to arrive.

"So, tell me a little about yourself. You ever been married?"

"No, as you can probably tell, I don't like men. And, well, I just haven't found the right person yet," Stalworth replied. "And you?"

"I was engaged to a wonderful woman once, but things didn't work out as planned. It was much easier for both of us to let go. Straight women that I know actually have a much harder go of it."

Stalworth's expression turned more serious. "It's such a bummer when that happens in life. I guess we just have to move on when it does," she replied.

"So true."

Hagenstock took a quick sip of her cocktail, lowering the glass as her eyes met Stalworth's. "So, tell me, now that we're here alone, what are some of your favorite fantasies? What kinky things do you like to do?"

"Well, I've always fantasized about meeting an attractive young lady, much like you, getting her alone and, well, doing naughty things to her."

Hagenstock smiled. "Okay, you've got me curious now. Like what? I want to hear it. What kind of things?"

"I'm embarrassed."

"Don't be. I don't kiss and tell."

"Actually, to be honest, I'd rather show than tell."

Hagenstock broke out into a hearty chuckle. "Okay, I like that. Well, we don't have to waste any more time here. Besides, I have a 10 a.m. start tomorrow. I'm filling in for my boss who's out on maternity leave," she said.

After the meeting, Stalworth walked the young woman out of the restaurant toward Wells Street, to the parking garage where she had parked her car.

While walking to Stalworth's vehicle, Hagenstock suddenly had an uneasy and eerie feeling come over her. She had always met with other women at hotel rooms, but never had the courage to go to someone else's apartment.

As the two walked through the dimly lit parking garage, Hagenstock stumbled slightly, trying hard to maintain her balance. Her speech slurred. "I have to admit one thing. I shouldn't have downed all those deliciously tasty damn cocktails. That much I know for sure. I'll be paying for it with one bitch of a hangover in the morning. But at least it'll be worth my while tonight, right?"

"Yes. Absolutely. This will be a night you won't soon forget," Stalworth quipped, offering a smile. "Please, let me open that door for you, sweetheart."

Stalworth opened the door to her SUV for the woman, then patiently waited, holding it like a parking valet at a five-star restaurant.

As Hagenstock began to clumsily climb into the passenger seat, Stalworth pounced, blanketing her nose and mouth with a cotton pad doused with chloroform. Hagenstock, eyes filled with terror, arms flailing, breathing in the deadly chemical, quickly crumpled into Stalworth's arms. Stalworth managed to tug her limp body into the vehicle before peeling away.

TAYLOR HAGENSTOCK'S PARENTS knew something was awry when their daughter failed to call or show up at work on Thursday morning.

In the city's cool predawn darkness, her nude and pallid corpse was found in a blue dumpster behind Empirical Furniture by several maintenance workers, who, after overcoming their initial shock, quickly called 911 to report the ghastly discovery.

Chicago police arrived within minutes and taped off the perimeter with yellow tape to prevent any passersby from contaminating the crime scene. Local reporters and news vans from CBS, NBC, ABC and WGN hurriedly descended on the block, as well as looky-loos from office buildings surrounding the area.

"Stay back," Chicago homicide detective Howard Beuregard barked at several bystanders as he exited his unmarked car and walked across the street to take in a closer view of the body. Beuregard was a seasoned veteran with numerous accolades to his credit during his twenty-three years of service and counting.

Pedestrians, blocked from walking near the crime scene, grew impatient, even belligerent. Beuregard turned from assessing the situation and abruptly stopped a young couple trying to meander their way through.

"Dude, my pregnant girlfriend's got a doctor's appointment across the street, and we need to get over there asap. It's urgent," said a spiked-hair rebellious type who looked like he could have fronted a wild heavy metal band.

"Well, your appointment is gonna wait!" the detective snapped back.

"Yeah? Well, thanks for the compassion, officer. I wonder if you'd say the same if she was one of *your* family members!"

"Look, asshole, we've got a murder here. *A murder.* I would say that takes priority over her doctor's appointment. And you want to talk shit to me about having compassion? Keep it up, and you and your girlfriend here will be wearing metal bracelets and spending the rest of the day in an eight-by-six lockup!"

"Whatever," the rocker mumbled beneath his breath.

Beuregard suddenly wheeled around and walked closer to the other cops and homicide detectives at the scene.

"Fellas, we got murders downtown now?" he called out to several patrolmen standing by.

"Well, we've got one."

Beuregard trudged closer and stood next to several crime scene techs, gazing in horror at Hagenstock's body lying amid piles of recyclable trash.

He shook his head. "Dammit! She looks so young and innocent. There are no defensive wounds or marks on her hands, feet or body. The ME's office should be arriving any minute. Keep the rest of those idiots across the street from coming over. We need to preserve this at all costs."

Hagenstock lay on her back, legs and arms splayed, her corpse semi-covered with scrap material, plastic and cardboard.

Her eyes were shiny and flat, frozen in time, still wide with fear from her untimely death that fateful night. Locks of her hair had been cut and her face had turned a horrid, bluish purple. There was a slight dribble of sticky fluid leaking from the right-hand corner of her mouth.

"Who found her?" Beuregard asked a uniformed cop on the scene.

"Some maintenance guys. They work at this place, Empirical Furniture. According to their witness statements, they were taking out the garbage after unpacking half a dozen sofas, and discovered the body when they opened the top of the dumpster."

"Anybody identify her?"

"Her wallet and driver's license were found on the ground in front of the container. Her murderer could have left them there or dropped them accidentally. Either way, Taylor Hagenstock's her name."

"I want as much surveillance video as we can get from businesses in the area. That's the first step, as usual. Has her family been notified?"

"Working on that now, Detective."

"Good. You guys are on the ball. The mayor's going to have major heat up our asses on this one. It's too close to home, if you know what I mean. I'm sure they're approving overtime as we speak."

"Gotcha. We're on it. Guys are canvassing the area now."

The buzz among the media hounds standing by echoed the inconvenient truth that it was highly unusual for such a crime to occur downtown, in the heart of the city, brazenly close to the rich and powerful and the most popular tourist attractions.

The mayor was in constant contact with Chicago's police superintendent, who put pressure on his top detectives to find answers. Quick.

Several miles away, Sarah Stalworth stayed holed up in her apartment, gripped by one of her maddening bouts of bipolar disorder, conveniently enjoying the luxury of not having to go out, as authorities sought to determine whether Hagenstock's murder was a targeted crime, or if she was the first victim of a deranged serial killer.

Her gaze was fixed on a nearby television, watching as special news reports interrupted regularly scheduled programming to discuss details of the grisly finding. "Lovely," she muttered as she zeroed in on every word that left the shaken, live-on-the-scene reporter's mouth.

She felt a rush of excitement. It was exhilarating and hilarious all at the same time. Moving to sit facing her computer, she turned toward the softly playing music in the distant background, the Gary Jules song, "Mad World."

She sang along hauntingly, "It's a very, very… mad world… mad world," as she adjusted her wig and removed the silk blouse from her large frame.

Suddenly, Stalworth stood from her office chair and strolled across the spacious room to look out of the apartment's living room window.

She peered in both directions, furtively surveying the tree-lined block. She was savvy enough to know that the police kept some information close to the vest. She would work hard to remain out of sight, for now.

She moved about this morning unflinching. Her pulse was still hammering. And she'd been smart enough *not* to bring Hagenstock back to her apartment.

"Nope, can't be that damn dumb! Not a chance!" she mumbled as she sat once again in her worn leather task chair, adjusting the height of her monitor, brightening the screen before she logged on to the internet.

There was more work to do, she thought. *A lot more to do.* This was only the beginning.

She ran the palm of her hand over the photos adorning the plaster wall alongside the computer. Each photograph was accompanied by a lock of hair from each victim. Her apartment had become a shrine to all the young women like the naive Taylor Hagenstock.

She despised them all, actually. Their pictures were neatly organized, from one side of the room to the other, all printed from their profile pages on the erotic chatroom web site which she had visited every night, looking for another helpless hack to murder.

She just had to know what they looked like. It was a simple rule. If there was no picture attached to a young woman's profile, the would-be sap did not exist, and the "unfit" prey would live to chat another day.

Stalworth *was* clever. Wickedly smart. She knew the type of mindfuck tricks that would make the most depraved of psychopaths blush with envy.

ACKNOWLEDGMENTS

I would like to thank God for his many blessings, a heartfelt thanks to my wife and my parents for their valuable feedback, my children and family for their love and support. A big thanks to my in-laws for supporting my endeavors, and many thanks to my readers for your continued support.

ABOUT THE AUTHOR

ALEX DEAN is the author of Restraining Order, The Bogeyman Next Door and Stalked. He is an entrepreneur, former musician, and self-proclaimed health enthusiast who enjoys being creative. He writes thrillers as well as other sub-genres of fiction and lives in Illinois with his family. For previews of his upcoming books and more information about Alex Dean, please visit alexdeanauthor.com.

If you want to get an automatic email when Alex's next book is released, you can sign up at alexdeanauthor.com. Your email address will never be shared and you can unsubscribe at any time. Word-of-mouth is crucial for any author to succeed. If you enjoyed this book, please consider leaving a review at Amazon.com, even if it's only a line or two; it would make all the difference and would be greatly appreciated.

OTHER WORKS BY ALEX DEAN

Alexis Fields Thrill Series

Book 1 - Restraining Order (An E-Original Short Story)

Alexis Fields is in the prime of her life, has just finished medical school and is celebrating her dream of becoming a doctor. But things go terribly wrong when she ends a volatile relationship with a disturbed man, Wilfred "Will" Bachman. Unable to handle the rejection, he develops a twisted obsession and promises to turn her life into a living hell.

After a vicious assault and a neighbor is found brutally murdered, the city of Madison is on edge. Top Madison Police Detective Lou Haney arrives on the scene and makes every effort to discover who the murderer might be. The city known as one of the best places to live has been thrown into chaos. Now Alexis has become a critical target as Bachman goes hell-bent on "revenge" before the police can find him. Will Alexis be able to escape her deranged ex? Will the police be able to solve the gruesome murder?

RESTRAINING ORDER is the beginning of Alex Dean's scariest, most chilling series yet.

Book 2 - The Bogeyman Next Door
Book 3 - Stalked

UPCOMING RELEASES

The Secret Life of Lula Darling

Lula Darling is a young girl growing up with her mother and younger brother on a Natchez, Mississippi plantation during slavery, until one day, she makes a startling discovery, one that magically transports her through time into the future, the place…Chicago.

Her life takes on new meaning when she meets and befriends another young girl named Ariel, whose parents' warm embrace offers Lula hope against formidable odds, and ultimately, allows her to become a positive and shining example to the youth of today. The Secret Life of Lula Darling is an inspirational, heartwarming story of the triumph of the human spirit, an unlikely friendship, and the appreciation of life that should be shared by all!

Gamer

The City of Chicago has seen an alarming number of murders over the summer. But the stakes are about to go much higher when a sadistic and deranged killer goes on a spree injuring thousands of people during large sporting events around the city. And only one man is thought capable of stopping him before things get even worse.

Special Agent Preston Ponder of the FBI's elite Violent Crime Apprehension Unit (VCAU) has been requested on the case. The incredibly handsome Ponder, with his supernatural instincts and highly advanced crime-fighting technology, is the city's only hope against the psychopathic killer known as *Gamer.*

www.ingramcontent.com/pod-product-compliance
Lightning Source LLC
Chambersburg PA
CBHW050948120626
46552CB00001B/431